Never Hug a Nun

a novel

by

Kevin Killeen

Blank Slate Press
Saint Louis, Missouri

Blank Slate Press

adventures in publishing
www.blankslatepress.com

[Blank Slate Press was founded in 2010 to discover, nurture, publish, and
promote new voices from the greater Saint Louis region and beyond.]

Published in the United States by Blank Slate Press, Saint Louis, Missouri 63110. No part of
this book may be reproduced, scanned, or distributed in any printed or electronic form without
written permission from the publisher, Blank Slate Press, LLC. Please do not participate in or
encourage piracy of copyrighted materials in violation of the author's rights.

This is a work of fiction. Any resemblance to actual events or locales or persons, living or dead,
is merely coincidental, and names, characters, places, and incidents are either the products of
the author's imagination or are used fictitiously.

Cover design Kristina Blank Makansi & Jane Colvin
Interior design by Kristina Blank Makansi

Library of Congress Control Number: 2012948119
ISBN: 978-0-9850071-0-2

PRINTED IN THE UNITED STATES OF AMERICA

To Nancy, thanks for marrying me
and having all those babies. I know ... I owe you.

Never Hvg a Nvn

spring

- chapter one -

THE NUN FIRED A WARNING GLANCE around the first-grade class-room. "Listen up," she said as she clicked on the projector and her doughy face floated in the light slicing up through the top of the slide carousel. "Today you're going to learn how God made the universe and everyone here out of utter nothingness." The children got quiet. The nun took a deep breath. It was a lot of work, creation, and this was her twenty-ninth year restaging the event.

Click. Click. The nun advanced the slides. "You're about to see what every-thing looked like *before* God created anything," she said.

Students leaned forward to learn this hidden truth. The only sound was the whir of the projector's cooling fan. Eyes widened. Toes tensed inside tasseled shoes and penny loafers. *Click. Click.* The first slide was supposed to show a dim slate of unending nothingness. But over Christmas break, a wool fiber from a nun's holiday scarf had drifted in there. It trembled in the fan breeze like a serpent. Outraged, the nun jabbed a number two pencil in the slide carousel to dislodge it. Students watched the battle play out on the screen as the fiber wriggled out of reach, defying the nun's swordsmanship. She stopped and looked at the screen, as if defeated, then launched a second, even more lethal attack, huffing and puffing around the projector, attempting to outflank the fiber from the left. She jabbed the pencil with the zeal of an archangel. But it was no use. The fiber refused to surrender. The nun sighed, put down her pencil, and clicked ahead to the next slide.

"And the Lord said, 'Let there be light,'" she intoned.

Sitting in the second row, third seat from the window, Patrick Cantwell wasn't paying any attention. He had discovered something far more interesting than creation, something he was feeling for the very first time. It was a feeling that made him wonder what was happening to him. It was an all new thing. On the surface, he looked incapable of the new thing. Too young, too much like his classmates—locked in lines of khaki, plaid and pine. But in the darkness of the slide show, his mind—and his heart—wandered.

He looked at the girl.

The nun saw him looking at the girl. She cleared her throat and Patrick looked back at the slide show. He tried to pay attention, but this production was worse than a Japanese monster movie. It was fake and impractical. For one thing, why would Adam take a nap half-naked in the mud, covered with only a few leaves here and there, which could be poison ivy, and, on top of that, risk waking up with ants and spiders crawling up his nose? If he'd had any sense, he would've made a hammock like they had on *Gilligan's Island* and not slept on the ground.

"And the Lord God built the rib which he took from Adam into a woman," the nun explained.

Patrick looked back at the girl.

Ebby Hamilton was sitting in the desk next to his, writing her name on a piece of paper—in cursive. Wow. He and the other first-graders only knew how to print. But it was not her penmanship that made him shiver as if he had just swallowed cough syrup. Maybe it was her black hair streaked with light brown, her smart eyes intent on her cursive letters, her no-good-for-sports stick arms, her plaid jumper and green socks in brown tassel shoes. Despite the way he usually felt like burping around girls, his mind ran away with her to the golf course. He was with her on the fairway by the railroad tracks, holding her fingertips, dancing with her in big, wide circles. It was the new thing, and it was breathtaking.

"And the Lord saw that it was good," the nun said. "Tomorrow we'll have the fall of Adam and Eve."

The final bell rang. It was three o'clock. The fluorescent ceiling lights flickered on with an institutional hum, and children sprang up row by row to get their windbreakers and metal lunch boxes from the cloakroom. Patrick tried to sit still and wait his turn, but he was fidgety and worried. Was she really going to do it? Would she really do *that?*

Patrick had been studying her. In the lunchroom, on the playground and in class, he had overheard and observed much about her without being noticed.

Once, they even drank from the double drinking fountain together. Their faces, just inches apart, were red from an April recess, when suddenly a slender loop of her hair swooped near his mouth. He gulped the water and wondered what to say when they came up for air. But she wiped her mouth and walked away. Nothing came of it.

Today was different. He had to gather the courage to talk to her. Otherwise … well, there was no otherwise. Her plan was just too dangerous. He had to stop her.

"Don't forget to practice printing Q, R, S, T, U, V," the nun said. "And I want to see a difference between your U's and V's. No sagging bottoms."

Girls chattered out the door, then down the steps and out into the sunshine. Finally, his turn came, and he headed for the door, but ended up stuck in a logjam of slow boys in ratty blue sweaters. He grabbed his metal *Wonderful World of Disney* lunch box, pushed his way through the crowd and ran down the steps outside.

"Hey, no running!" yelled a crew-cut Webelo patrol guard. Patrick ignored him and sped down the sidewalk.

Something changed in the solar system at three o'clock. Everyone was liberated, happier than they'd been just two minutes earlier. Hundreds of girls in green plaid, boys in khaki and white with blue neckties streamed away from the school. They screamed and laughed as they ran. Papers flew. Schwinns with baseball cards flapping on the spokes rolled by. An orange school bus hunched and squeaked, kids bouncing on its seats. The science teacher who was not a nun tried to start her Volkswagen Beetle while the cafeteria lady lugged out another sack of milk pennies to deposit at the bank. Everyone fled. Everyone felt the change. Everyone except the piano students who marched like lifers to the nun's stone house to practice their scales.

Patrick hopped over some Vatican-style bushes and ran past the church rummage sale sign toward Ebby, who was already flying across the front steps of the church. Her path crossed the afternoon shadow cast from the giant gold-plated statue of Mary on the church roof. She ran past the janitor who, in anticipation of the coming Easter festivities, dripped gasoline from a red can onto the spring's first sidewalk weeds. Then she ducked her head and disappeared through the arching hedge line that marked the end of the church property.

The janitor kept pouring gasoline as he watched Patrick run after the girl. He shook his head and offered up a Hail Mary. Shooting through the hedge, Patrick saw her flying down the sidewalk toward the train bridge. He ran faster.

Pepsi cans, dead leaves, and decayed school papers blurred underfoot, and as he ran, he could hear it—the afternoon freight train. The engine sounded serious. He could see it approaching, spewing out blue-black smoke, leaning forward toward the bridge as if racing the girl to the finish line. Patrick caught up with her, and their shoes slapped the sidewalk—*clap clop, clap clop, clap clop*—like the horses in *Ben Hur*.

"Don't do it," he yelled. "My dad says you can get killed up there."

"Have to! She's having it today," she yelled back.

At the bottom of the embankment leading up to the bridge, he stopped. She ran ahead of him, scrambling up the gravel path toward the top. He looked to the left. The train was nearing the far side of the bridge. His dad had told him to never ever *ever* go up there on the tracks. The train thundered onto the bridge. It would be a sin, his dad warned, a sin against the commandment to Honor Your Father and Mother. He watched Ebby climb with her skinny legs. His heart went after her, and his legs followed.

Dropping his lunch box on the sidewalk, he ran up the hill. Gravel slipped under his penny loafers. Afraid and panting, he grabbed onto the weeds to pull himself higher. The engines shook the bridge. The horn blasted. She was at the top, flexing her knees. She looked back at him.

"C'mon," she yelled. He caught up and reached out for her just as she jumped. Her pleated uniform skirt filled with air as she leaped across the tracks. He closed his eyes and jumped after her. He was airborne, like he was jumping the Grand Canyon. Faced with certain death, he wondered what his Mom was cooking for dinner. Would it be good? Maybe pizza or hamburgers? Or would it be gross? Like the beef stew he and his brothers called beef poo?

The engine missed him by sixteen inches. A violent pocket of air threw him to the side, and he landed, sprawling in the rocks beside the girl. The horn stopped, but the blast still rang in his ears.

"I wished for a sister!" she yelled. She jumped up, shook her fist at the train and laughed.

The engineer stuck his head out the side window and looked back at them. His cap blew off. Patrick and Ebby waved to him, but the engineer shook his fist back at them and opened his monkey-wrench jaw to curse them. They couldn't hear him over the engines, and besides, they didn't care what he had to say. They had done it. They had jumped the tracks and survived.

But the anger of the train made the ground quake and the skin on their faces vibrate. Rushing air tore through the tall grass and blew back their hair.

Coal cars raged forward, yellow and gritty, wheels thumping and slicing along the rails. The wooden ties dipped up and down in the rock roadbed. It was a huge train, a half-mile column of rolling death and they had mocked it.

"We shouldn't have done it," he yelled.

"I hope I get my wish," she shouted.

"What do you mean, get your wish?"

She cupped her hands to his ears. They were warm and her soft voice poured into his brain like maple syrup on a stack of pancakes.

"I can't have another brother," she said. "I hate my brother. He hit me for breaking his stupid model car, and when he got grounded, I told him I wished he was dead and wished for a sister to take over his stupid room. He told me I'd never get a sister, because the only way to get a wish for sure is to jump in front of a train at the exact same time you say your wish."

She backed away from him and shook her fist again at the train. "Hah. I did it. He'll see. When it's a girl, he'll see."

Together they watched the coal cars and caught their breath in the warm, train air. He turned to study her, the way her brown eyes squinted as the wind blew her hair in swirls around her head. Her hair tangled in her tapered fingers as she tried to move it off her face. He wanted to hold her hand.

"What do you wish for?" she said.

He knew it was a lie, that she had been deceived. You couldn't get a wish by jumping in front of a train, especially since it was a sin to even be on the tracks. But he couldn't tell her that. He glanced at his pants and noticed they were filthy. He thought of his Mom, and was ashamed. She was the one who made everyone in the family try to be good and wear clean underwear.

"C'mon, tell me, what you wish for."

"I guess, I just want to go to heaven someday," he said.

A defective coal car rattled by. "You have to wish for something *real*, like a bike," she shouted. She stood up and jabbed her hands toward the wheels to tease the train. The train couldn't reach her, so she laughed. "I've got to go and find out if it's a girl!" He lay in the grass and watched Ebby leave. She slid down the other side of the embankment through the weeds, and skipped down the sidewalk, not looking both ways as she crossed the street. Her hair bounced and she got smaller as she disappeared down Main Street.

Patrick looked back at the train. It was going faster. Coal cars rocked from side to side. They smelled oily, like the trashcans from a hundred gas stations. He knew the caboose would be coming, so he covered himself in the tall weeds.

Kevin Killeen

His Dad had warned him about how caboose men shoot rifles with rock salt at boys they see on the tracks. The caboose passed. The after-wind tugged at the trees and shook the leaves as it whooshed around the curve and sucked all the noise with it. He stood up.

He ran and picked up the engineer's cap and put it on. He stood there in his cap and looked at the forbidden bridge. The word SHIT was spray-painted on the inside walls. He read it for the first time. His tongue touched the roof of his mouth as he said it, twice. SHIT. SHIT. It meant nothing. His eyes ran over the purple weeds and the scrub brush that grew up along the tracks as far as he could see. In the distance, he could see the golf course fairway where he had imagined dancing with her. He took a deep breath and felt the new thing. But then he looked again at his dirty pants and grass-stained white shirt. He realized he would have to sneak in the house, that he'd have to get his pants past Mom.

He hid the engineer's cap in some weeds, and went down the hill to get his lunch box. But it was dented and scratched and reminded him of what he had done wrong. He threw it in the bushes and ran home.

8

- chapter two -

HIS MOM PULLED ANOTHER TRAY of Tollhouse cookies from the oven when Patrick eased open the front door of their three-story Victorian home. He winced as the door squeaked, and then tiptoed past hallway photos of relatives watching him—his aunt who was a nun, and his Mom's dead dad with the purgatory card on his picture frame.

"That you, Patrick?" his mom called from the kitchen.

"Yeah, Mom, I'm gonna change," he yelled as he sprinted upstairs before she could come out and catch him.

She flipped the perfect cookies with a spatula onto the cooling rack and wondered why Patrick came in the front door and not the back. And why didn't he come straight to the kitchen with the smell of warm cookies in the air? With three boys, she could never be too suspicious. But she let it go and hummed along with the big band song playing on the radio. It was Tex Beneke and the Modernaires with the Glenn Miller orchestra.

She smiled as the music carried her back to 1947 when she was the prettiest girl at Ursuline Academy. Counter stools swiveled when she walked into the Parkmoor sandwich shop after a movie with one of her dates. She could feel the eyes—both admiring and jealous—as she crossed the room with her shoulder-length red hair bouncing, her slim figure, and a face like a girl on a Coca-Cola tray. Her dating years were just beginning, and before they would end, she would have gone out with 108 young men. Other girls fretted they might never hear the words from their favorite love songs, but she heard so many lyrics, and so soon, that she started rehearsing new ways to say no. Boys who dreamed of being doctors, lawyers and downtown men sat across candle-lit tables and offered her velvet-covered boxes holding sparkling promises of everlasting love and solid financial futures. They all wanted to be with her, but she kept her distance, and more, by giving innocent Doris Day smiles and by letting the phone ring the next day until her father answered it to say she's not home and where do you go to church.

True love—her widowed, Irish father Patrick O'Hanlon had told her after waiting up for her one night—was a gift. That night she found him sitting at the piano, hat slanted over his careworn forehead, playing a five-cent song from his own sweetheart days, "Meet Me Tonight in Dreamland." As he played, he looked at his wedding photo hanging on the wall. It had been taken in 1919, and he was wearing his World War I uniform. His eyes were beaming in the photo, but as he sat at the piano that needed tuning, he was old, and his eyes were sad and tired, like a doughboy whose leave was almost over and the Argonne Forest was waiting.

She listened to her father play as she sat in her party dress, straightened her pleats, and relived the date that had just ended. His hands moved across the keys in the dim lamplight and then the song faded away, and he turned toward her. God, he said, reaching for a glass of O.F.C. Whiskey, was going to lead her to fall in love with a man who would really love her. And that man would be Catholic, and together they would raise a fine Catholic family.

"Patrick, what are you doing up there?" she yelled up the laundry chute.

"Just changing."

"What's the water running for?"

"Trying to get clean."

Something was up. But she didn't feel like climbing the steps to find out.

The back door swung open and Patrick's older brother, John, walked in. John was one of the coolest kids at Mary Queen of Our Hearts School. For a second-grader, John was smart, good looking and advanced. He already knew what he wanted in life. It was 1966 and John wanted to become a Beatle. Specifically, he wanted to become John Lennon. Since realizing his purpose, he walked more confidently, like a boy with an atomic secret. His only problem, which he kept to himself, was that he did not own, or know anything about, a guitar.

"Hi, John," Mom said.

"'ello, Mum."

"I made cookies."

"Fab," he said, checking the mirror by the refrigerator. The back door opened again, and Teddy came in carrying sheets of construction paper with crayon and milk stains from the afternoon pre-school. Teddy ran right to Mom, and she leaned down to his level to kiss him. Teddy was the skinny, quiet boy who almost died of spinal meningitis a year ago. Now he was four-and-a-half and showing an interest in sports. But he was still too weak to really punch around.

"Oh, Teddy, you're the *last one* home, and the *first one* to kiss me." She looked toward the back porch. "You hear that, John?"

John was in front of the mirror, analyzing a bang that had potential, all the while lightly singing a few lines from the Beatles' tune, "Boys."

"John! Quit looking at yourself and come over here," Mom said.

John went over and hugged his Mom, and she sneaked a kiss on his cheek. In her presence—her warm apron and the cookie fumes—he left Liverpool briefly and spoke to her in his own voice. "Hi, Mom."

"That's better. Here, you boys have some cookies while I get some more out of the oven. And drink some milk."

"Can we have soda?" Teddy asked.

"No, remember we gave up soda for Lent," Mom said. "I wonder what that Patrick is up to."

Upstairs, Patrick was in his underwear sprinkling Lysol Tub and Tile Cleaner on his pants and shirt. On the sink before him was an array of products—Barbasol Shaving Cream, Tucks Pads and Preparation H. But nothing was working. Frustrated, he finally ditched his dirty clothes under his bed and pulled on his straight-legged blue jeans with cuffs, a green plaid shirt, and white Keds. Walking downstairs, he passed the front hallway photos of his aunt who was the nun and the dead grandfather he was named after. Their eyes followed him around the corner to where Mom was waiting in the kitchen.

"Patrick, are you in trouble?"

"No."

She looked into his eyes. His eyes were hard to understand. Once he had dropped lit matches down the clothes chute and set Dad's executive underwear on fire. But when she asked him about that one, he admitted it. He had not yet fallen into the sin of lying.

"What happened today?"

The speeding freight train shot through his mind. "Nothing."

She looked at him.

He knew he'd better say something. "We had a slide show." She slapped the gooey batter on the tin tray with a wooden spoon to the beat of Big Band Radio. The music oozed through the kitchen like strands of chocolate from a pulled-apart cookie. Nearby, in the breakfast room, a competing song blared from the black and white TV.

The cartoon *Speed Racer* was on. Patrick saw John and Teddy enjoying the show with cookies and milk and wanted to join them. He wanted to escape his Mom's questions before he confessed everything.

"Patrick, I know something."

He saw himself diving in front of the train. "Is it something good?"

"Somebody called you, right before you came home."

He thought of the engineer with his head out the window. Maybe there was a phone on the train like on boats. "Who was it?"

"Patrick, my number-two son, my son named after my dear Daddy, to think seven years ago you weren't even *alive*."

"Yeah." He looked at the cookies and fought the urge to run.

"It's quite a thing to be alive. It's an un-asked for thing. It's … you ever stop to think you might not have been born? Your father could have married somebody else. Or I could have married somebody else." He felt like running from the house, running around the block, peeing on a bush, but she had him in an eye lock. "Yes … I married your father, and you came from us, and at just the only possible time for you to be, you *were*. And now here you are in the first grade at Mary Queen of Our Hearts, studying catechism and getting a call from … *a girl!*"

Ebby! Ebby had called his house. She must have told his Mom everything, and he would probably be grounded forever. He looked at Mom to see what his punishment would be. But her eyes were not punishing. They were believing— the way they believed when Dad remembered their wedding anniversary with a last-minute trip to the Rexall Drugstore greeting card section.

She straightened his hair. He kept looking at the cookies.

"Well, what's she like?"

He thought of Ebby's shiny hair blowing in the train wind, and her fingers trying to keep it off her face. "I don't know."

"You must know something about her."

He remembered her smart, brown eyes, the way they lit up when she was writing in cursive. "She can write her name in handwriting."

"Is she pretty?"

He looked to the side, embarrassed. "Yes."

"What do you think she wants? I mean, calling you, *a girl calling a boy.*"

"I don't know. Her mom is having a baby today."

"Today?"

"Yeah."

She hugged him. "Today, *of all days.* Life is like a song."

- chapter three -

LIFE WAS TIRESOME AND DREARY for the dads who worked downtown. They drove there from the suburbs Monday through Friday, wearing uniform suits and ties. As they drove, the trees parted and the Gateway Arch sprouted on the horizon. The brand new, 630 foot tall, stainless steel Arch was a sensation honoring the early explorers who had escaped St. Louis. While Lewis and Clark had braved the unknown to map the West, modern dads pulled their cars into yellow-lined parking spaces, stepped into crowded elevators, and surrendered themselves to office buildings resembling above-ground mine shafts. Some of the dads had windows and could enjoy the view with their morning coffee. They looked out and saw other dads holding coffee mugs in other office buildings, or watched the Mississippi glittering behind the Arch on its way to the gulf and the freight trains burdened with heavy loads, creaking across the bridges and out of town. Some dads wished they could run from the building and jump in the river, or hop a train and go somewhere. They wished they could be free of their jobs, sleeping every morning until they ran out of sleepiness, eating ham and eggs in their pajamas without shaving, reading the sports page from front to back like everyday was a Saturday.

But their boyhoods were spent. Now they were men. They owed money to the bank for their houses, money to the grocery store for their food, money to Union Electric for all the lights their kids always left burning. In debt from all sides, they had to provide for their growing families. And every day was a fight to keep going. Now, at five o'clock, they climbed back into their mine shaft elevators, pulled out of their yellow-lined parking spaces, and turned their cars back toward the suburbs where wives and children and yards and bills waited for them. And all the while they thought about how their bosses yelled at them and how they had to perform the same routine the next day and the next and the next after that.

"*Because I've had a miserable day,*" Dad told Mom, "*that's* why I don't want to listen to Big Band Radio." Dad put down his briefcase in the living room, and sat in his World's Fair chair with duck down cushions and twirly woodwork. He took the Old Fashioned from Mom's hand and held it to his forehead.

"Thanks. Boy, what a day," Dad said.

Mom danced herself across the living room, hoping tonight would be different. She wanted the mood to be romantic, so she could tell Dad *the big news.* She clicked off the radio, and tried to distract him before he started complaining about the office. "Patrick got a phone call from a girl," she said flipping through her Frank Sinatra records.

"What year is it?" Dad said. He took another sip and studied her. She seemed as happy as a high school girl who had somehow wandered into adulthood. She had no idea what it was like in the Mergers and Acquisitions Department at St. Louis Foods.

St. Louis Foods, a rapidly expanding national corporation, was conquering the institutional food market—taking prisoner a five-gallon canned soup firm one week, then a just-add-water mashed potato company the next. And Dad was right in the middle of the battle. He was currently devising a secret plan to acquire the BOY IS IT GOOD Cake Mix Company.

"A phone call from a girl?" Dad said, "Where *are* the boys?"

"They all ran up to do their homework when they heard your car pull in," Mom said. She glanced at Dad as he stared at his framed lithograph of the *Battle of the Wilderness.* For some reason, the Civil War scene hanging above the chair where Mom usually sat fascinated him. Rifles blasting, men bleeding, horses falling in wild-eyed agony—his eyes would drift to it as Mom told stories about parish mothers she had seen at garage sales and retell jokes the announcer had made that day on Big Band Radio.

"You mind if I play this record?" she asked. She fingered her hair and held up the album cover of Frank Sinatra. Sinatra's hat was tilted carefree and he was snapping his fingers real coolbaby. Dad pulled his eyes away from the *Battle of the Wilderness* and looked at Sinatra.

"Oh, let's just have some quiet. I can't brook that gangster."

Mom said nothing as she slowly started to push the record back onto the shelf. But something in her manner reminded Dad of the way defeated dockworkers filed their time cards down at the St. Louis Foods warehouse.

"OK, *I'm sorry.* You're right. We should play the record," Dad said. He put down his drink and looked at her, his eyes all soft and apologetic.

Mom smiled at him the way she used to when they were dating, and Dad couldn't help himself. He smiled back. She put the record on, and hurried over to take Dad's hands before the music began.

He looked up at her from his chair. "You don't expect me *to dance,* do you?" She took his hands, pulled him to his feet, and placed his arms around her. She stood on tiptoes to kiss him. "Honey, I'm pregnant," she whispered.

Before he could say anything, an unexpected song blasted from the hi-fi speaker. Instead of Sinatra, it was the Monkees singing "The Last Train to Clarksville." As usual, the boys had jammed their record into the wrong album cover during a rushed clean-up.

"That's great. That's terrific, you're doing a terrific job," he said as the surprise flooded his mind like a flurry of memos from the workers' union.

"Aren't you going to say you love me?"

"Of course, you know that."

John, Patrick, and Teddy ran downstairs to see who was playing their Monkees record. They stopped at the banister and watched. Mom had slipped out of her shoes, her arms were wrapped around Dad's neck, and her face was pressed into his chest. A small smile played on her lips, and her eyes were closed as she thought of the baby. Maybe it would be a girl.

Dad's eyes were wide open as he stared at the *Battle of the Wilderness* and thought about his mounting responsibilities. He tried to keep his downtown shoes off her toes as Union and Confederate soldiers shot each other in the face.

- chapter four -

THE KITCHEN PHONE HUNG ON THE WALL like a ticking time bomb. All through dinner, Patrick worried about Ebby's phone call. It was bad enough not knowing how to call her back or what to say. He had never talked to a girl on the phone before. His brother John had pointed out once that he said *um* too much and sounded stupid. Now he was worried that she might call him during dinner with his family listening, and he would end up saying, *um, um, um.*

"Patrick, you're not eating," Dad said, sipping his milk. "You must have a lot on your mind." Patrick looked at Mom and glanced at the phone. Dad scanned the table and noticed his youngest moving food around on his plate. "Teddy, your string beans."

"They're *gross*," Teddy said.

"Yes, I know, they're gross," Dad said. He lowered his voice to the special hospital hush he'd used with Teddy since the meningitis. "But, you see, Ted, string beans make you strong so you won't get sick again. I'll play catch with you after dinner if you eat them."

Teddy's cheeks flushed like he might cry, but he thought of playing catch, and forced the disgusting, cold string beans in his mouth.

"That's my boy," Dad said. He turned his attention to his oldest son, John, who had wetted back his lengthening bangs to conceal his Beatle ambitions. Dad wore a business haircut and had once purchased a home barber kit at Mac Hardware to save money on the boys. Dad's first experiment had made John cry, so Mom hid the barber kit up high on the closet shelf. "John, I read in the paper today that the Beatles are coming to Webster Groves. They're going to have a concert at the Velvet Freeze."

"*Dad!*" John said.

"Actually, I did read that they're coming to St. Louis."

John studied Dad to see if it was a joke, but Dad looked serious as he chewed.

"Are they *really* coming?"

"I read they're coming in August. They're going to perform at the new baseball stadium."

"Can we go?" John blurted, sitting up straight.

Mom answered for him. "John, *really*, you're only in second grade. The Beatles are for teenagers. Besides, I heard an editorial on Big Band Radio that said the Beatles think they're better than God." The dog cruised under the table looking for scraps. Teddy surreptitiously held out a few wilted green beans for him. "I don't think they're a good influence," Mom continued. She looked at Dad for support. She wanted him to say a few Catholic words, but Dad was not the kind of Catholic to make speeches. He separated his applesauce from his pork butt and changed the subject.

"So John, what did you learn in school today?" Dad asked.

"Nothing, just more long division," John said, "It's stupid."

"Long division isn't stupid," Dad said. "You'll use that all your life when you grow up and work downtown in business."

Mom perked up. "And what about … *multiplication?*"

Dad smiled at her. She smiled back. They both drank some milk. The two older boys knew something was up. Teddy, unaware, piled the rest of his string beans in his mouth and began chewing.

"Boys, your mother and I have some news tonight. She went to the doctor and found out we're going to have another baby.

Teddy swallowed and announced, "I'm finished with my string beans!"

"Great, Teddy, that's great. We'll play catch in just a minute. But did you hear what I just said? Your Mom is having a baby."

Mom raised her eyebrows and nodded.

Dad turned serious. "Men, listen now, your mother is going to carry the load on this for us. It's quite a thing. This means you'll all have to help more. Especially you two older boys. Set the example. Let's begin tonight by taking care of the dishes. And I think we should all clap for her."

They applauded and whooped and yelled "Go Mom" around their small table. Patrick clapped and hollered the loudest so that if the phone rang, no one would hear it.

- chapter five -

DAD AND TEDDY PLAYED CATCH in the backyard while Patrick and John cleared the dishes, and Mom rested in the living room. She reclined on the sofa and reached for something to read. *The St. Louis Review*, the weekly Catholic newspaper, was on top of the pile of books and magazines. An important source of religious news and ads for honest tree trimmers, *The Review* had been coming to the house for years. Mom always wanted its sermon-like presence prominently visible on the coffee table, but someone could have hidden a five-dollar bill inside, and it would have been safe. She scanned the front page and then quickly laid it aside and picked up the paperback *Baby and Child Care* by Dr. Benjamin Spock. The pages were worn and dog-eared, especially in the chapter on how to reason with children without having to spank them. After thumbing through a few pages, she laid it aside, looked out the window to see that Dad and Teddy were still in the backyard, and pulled out a James Bond novel hidden under the cushion.

James Bond was sweeping the parish. Mothers everywhere had been reading the adventures of the handsome, British secret agent. He was hairy chested, and his stomach was tan and flat. He wore clean shirts from an outside laundry service, swept women into his muscular arms, and kissed them right on the lips. When James Bond loved a woman, he did something about it, even if people were shooting at him from the next room. The fast-paced books never clearly stated whether 007 attended Mass regularly, but the mothers at Mary Queen of Our Hearts assured each other that Bond novels were "educational," and Bond kept them abreast of current events.

In the kitchen, Patrick jammed plates and glasses in the wrong compartments of the dishwasher. He kept looking at the phone on the wall. Would Ebby call? What would he say to her? He put the salt and pepper shakers in the dishwasher.

"*Hey, man*, salt and pepper doesn't get washed," John said. "I'll load. You clear the table."

Patrick carried in the pork butt platter, and John fixed the mess in the dishwasher. John turned to Patrick and whispered, "I wonder if it'll be a girl. I think Mom really wants a girl."

"You ever call a girl on the phone?" Patrick said.

"Sure."

"What's it like?"

"It's just one of those things."

"How do you know what to say?"

"When you call a girl? You just say what comes natural. Be yourself. But always write it out first. And it helps to play a good record in the background. You need to call on the upstairs phone by the mirror."

The kitchen phone rang. Patrick ran out the back door.

John glanced out the window, ran his fingers through his hair, and pulled his bangs back down over his forehead. "'Ello."

It was for John.

++++

In the back yard, Dad and Teddy threw a tennis ball back and forth with an intimacy rooted in Teddy's victory over meningitis. Dad remembered watching his frail boy vomit into trashcans as the bacteria attacked him. He had steadied Teddy's shoulders as they shook with fever, and, in a take-charge way, Dad had carried Teddy to the car for the 80-mile-an-hour race to the emergency room. The doctors said Dad's action had saved Teddy's life. The tennis ball left Dad's hand. It snapped in Teddy's glove and did not fall out.

Patrick sat on the stump of a dead tree and watched them play. It was warm, but the night chill was falling. The orange sky outlined the majestic oak trees that had probably been growing in their back yard since Indian boys and girls felt the new thing. Patrick looked at the telephone wire running to the house. He thought about how Ebby's voice had traveled across that wire earlier in the day.

"Dad, how old were you when you first called a girl on the phone?"

"*Good grief*, what a question. You shouldn't worry about that until you're in college. Forget about love. You want to play catch?"

"No, thanks," he said watching Teddy finger the ball. Patrick hated baseball, especially little league. The games were hot, dusty, bees-in-the-clover boring, with other dads yelling at Patrick to *use both hands. You're not a pro.* Dropped balls, strikeouts, bad throws, losses, defeat, bee stings, shame and infamy—the only good thing about little league was the post-game root beer.

Besides, sports had become a Dad and Teddy thing. Each son had to find his own thing to do alone with Dad. With Teddy, it was sports. With John, it was going to Webster Records on Saturday to buy a Monkees or a Beatles record. With Patrick, it was getting in trouble. Those private lectures Dad gave him after he got caught were always very relaxing. Dad would sit in his World's Fair chair with his suit and tie still on. Patrick would take the straight back chair in front of him. Dad would listen to Patrick's version of how ketchup got in a neighbor's central air unit, or how rocks came to jam another neighbor's automatic sprinkler system. Then Dad would clear his throat and whisper so Patrick's brothers listening from the steps could not hear. Dad would ask Patrick to "never do this sort of thing again." Patrick would nod and they would shake hands. Patrick's troubles seemed to bind them together.

Dad picked up the ball to throw to Teddy. The dog ran over to the stump where Patrick was sitting and he petted it. "Patrick, are the dishes done?" Dad said.

"Yes, sir."

"Don't call me sir. I want you boys to always just call me Dad."

"OK, Dad."

"Good work on the dishes. That's one thing I've learned downtown. When you have a job, you have to do good work. Remember that all your life."

Teddy struggled to throw the ball, his skinny arm whirring through the air in an elaborate wind-up.

"*Just think,*" Dad said to Teddy, "when the new baby comes, you won't be the youngest anymore."

Teddy leaned forward. The vitamins from his string beans flowed down his arm, and he whipped the ball as hard as he could. It sliced straight into the ivy bushes, and the dog bounded after it.

"That's enough for tonight. It's getting chilly, and it's time to get ready for bed, boys. Patrick, is your homework done?"

"I don't have any."

"*No homework?* When I went to *public* school, we always had homework. I don't know what those nuns are teaching you."

- chapter six -

PATRICK PICKED UP THE PHONE in the upstairs hallway and put it to his ear. The dial tone was loud and steady like the warning blast from the freight train. He took the Mary Queen of Our Hearts buzz book and opened it to the page with names beginning in "H." His finger marked the spot:

HAMILTON, CHARLES AND MARGARET... DAUGHTER, EBBY (1st GRADE), SON, RAVEN....

Seeing her name in print made him feel the new thing. He looked around to see if anyone was spying on him. He jumped as a voice suddenly began speaking to him.

"If you would like to make a call, please hang up and check to see that all your receivers are in place. There is trouble on your line. This is a recording. BEEP, BEEP, BEEP, BEEP...."

The beeping sound and the terror of calling a girl put his bladder on a broken dam alert. He slammed the receiver down, ran into the bathroom, and kicked the door shut behind him. Unzipping quickly, trigger hand shaking, he tinkled willy-nilly across the un-lifted seat, then took Dad's shower towel, wiped off the splatter, and hung it back up.

Now he was ready to call Ebby. With a deep breath, he opened the bathroom door. John was talking on the phone and looking at himself in the hallway mirror. The Beatles song, "Love, Love Me Do," was playing on the record player. *Whew!* Patrick exhaled a breath he didn't know he'd been holding.

"Hey, boys, it's 8:15. Get to bed," Dad yelled up the steps.

John hung up the phone, took one more close look at his bangs, and he and

Patrick started their bedtime routine. Patrick put on his Batman pajamas and climbed into the top bunk. John stripped down to his underwear.

"Aren't you going to put on your Superman pajamas?" Patrick said.

"No," John said, turning off the record player.

"You're going to sleep in your underwear?"

"Yeah," John said, getting out his transistor radio. "I want to sleep naked, to get a really good night sleep like Tarzan, but Mom caught me trying it and said I have to at least wear underwear."

"Why?"

"She said it's a sin to have nudity."

"What's nudity?"

"It's when you don't wear underwear."

Patrick lay on his back and looked at the ceiling. "Once, when I couldn't find any underwear, I went to school with nudity under my pants."

"That's not nudity. That's just *stoo*-piddy."

John turned on KXOK where DJ Johnny Rabbit was playing all the hits. With a white wire dangling between his radio and his earplug, he plopped onto the bottom bunk. Patrick stretched out and turned off the light switch with his big toe. John turned on his bedside lamp and flipped through a Beatles magazine. Patrick wanted to do something, too. Now that he didn't have to talk to a girl on the phone, he had all sorts of extra energy.

He reached for his Wolfman, a plastic model that his Granddad Cantwell had given to him. Patrick studied the teeth and the red blood paint on the Wolfman's fingers. Granddad had helped him paint it. Unlike the grandfather Patrick was named after, Granddad Cantwell was not dead. Granddad Cantwell spit and smoked cigars and breathed life into the family. Sometimes, Granddad didn't get along with Mom. Like buying the Wolfman model. Mom thought it was grotesque. But it wasn't. She didn't know. She had never seen the movie.

Granddad had taken the boys to see the Wolfman movie at the Ozark Theater. The Wolfman was a regular citizen in a suit and tie who tried to be good. But when there was a full moon, he killed people. Patrick respected that about the Wolfman. The Wolfman *tried* to be good. But if he couldn't be good, he didn't hold back. He killed a lot of people through no fault of his own.

The room was quiet. John cut a fart and fanned it up toward Patrick with his Beatles magazine.

"Gross!" Patrick yelled.

John buried his face in his pillow and laughed. To him, there was nothing funnier than a fart, except his own farts. From downstairs, Dad heard the commotion and yelled for them to *please get to sleep.* John turned off the lamp. Patrick laid aside the Wolfman. He hugged his pillow and thought of Ebby and what it would be like to really hold her hands and dance together on the golf course fairway.

- chapter seven -

EBBY'S DESK WAS EMPTY the next day. Patrick gazed over at it and imagined her hand holding a pen and writing in cursive on the slanted pine top. He pictured her plaid skirt and her knee-socked legs, one tucked under the other.

"Life is a mystery," the nun told the class. She turned out the lights and turned on the slide projector. "But *this* we do know … before The Fall, the earth was a paradise. It looked like this."

The students gasped as the slide clicked into place. It was a group of smiling nuns with blinding, white legs dangling over the edge of a bubbling mineral pool.

"Sorry, class, wrong slide. That's the convention in Eureka Springs."

Patrick looked over at Ebby's desk and wondered if she got her wish, if the new baby was a girl. The nun fixed the slide tray and went on.

"God breathed into Adam, and he became a living soul. Does anyone know what that means?"

Jimmy Purvis, a boy with a missing front tooth, waved his hand in the air. "Yes, Jimmy?"

He jumped up and stood proudly beside his desk. "It means breathing is important. We should never smoke unfiltered," Jimmy said. "My Dad smokes only Winston filtered."

"Sit down, Jimmy, that's not the right answer."

Jimmy sat down, disgraced, while the nun opened the window behind the shuttered venetian blinds. "Does anyone know the right answer?"

No one else raised a hand, but Patrick knew the answer. Mom had already put him to bed with all kinds of Catholic stories. He waited a moment, and then, reluctantly, raised his hand.

"Yes, Patrick?"

"It means Adam was made in God's image. It means he had a soul."

A little sigh of wind blew the venetian blinds away from the windowsill, brightening the room. Then the wind let go of them, and the blinds clanked back against the window and the room was dark again.

"Excellent! Patrick! Class, let's give Patrick our silent clappers." The students lightly patted their fingers on their palms, being careful not to make a clapping noise that might disturb the class next door. The nun smiled. "Patrick, come forward and receive your reward."

Patrick got up and walked around Ebby's desk. His fingertips drifted across the back of her chair as he passed. The nun continued.

"You see, children, the most important truth you'll ever learn in first grade, even more important than consonants and vowels, is that each of you has a soul." Patrick took the candy tin off her desk and popped the top off. "A soul is something that God gave each one of you before you were even born. It's what makes you more important than a tree or a dog."

Patrick struggled to see what type of candy was in the tin. But with the lights out, he needed to carry it over into the beam of the slide projector to help in his selection.

"So, you see," the nun said with her back to Patrick, "your soul is who you *really are* inside. It's an invisible person that will live forever, either in heaven if you're good, or if you're bad—"

Patrick was getting nowhere. He could see now that the tin contained nothing more than bargain butterscotches and nun mints. Determined, he began shaking the tin like a prospector panning for chocolate-covered caramel. The nun turned around.

"*Patrick Cantwell!* What's that noise? Haven't you taken your piece yet?"

He stopped. "No, Sister."

"Well, what's the problem?"

"Don't you have anything better?"

++++

At precisely 11:45, Patrick's class stood row by row. Those who had brought lunches got them out of the cloakroom, then they all walked quietly, single file, down the hallway. They passed the principal's office. The principal, a forty-year-old nun, was sitting behind her desk eating lumpy cottage cheese and reading an article on boyhood psychology. The class marched past the life-sized plaster statues of Joseph and Mary. They pivoted left between two glass cases containing the plastic gold trophies of the school's past sports teams. Then they walked down the steps and under the plaque engraved with the name of the boy who died sledding in 1954, before his first confession.

At the bottom of the second flight of steps, the lock-step line broke as the commotion of the cafeteria and the smell of institutional food overtook them. Those who had money got in line by the steam trays. They glided their plastic trays—still warm from the dishwasher—along the stainless steel rails, looking through the slanted glass at the hot food and the Mothers' Club volunteers. The volunteers served up fish rectangles, factory hamburgers made off site, super salty chicken noodle soup or, on Wednesday only, pepperoni pizza slices. Buying lunch was expensive. A good lunch cost nearly forty-five cents, or sixty cents if you wanted to throw in cheese popcorn, a pretzel stick or an Eskimo Pie. Patrick and the others who brought bag lunches got in the milk line. He paid Mrs. Heimlich, the heavy-set cafeteria lady, four pennies for a carton of milk. Mrs. Heimlich shook her head as the pennies she would later have to count and take to the bank piled up.

"Doesn't anybody have a nickel anymore?" she said.

The cafeteria was crowded. It featured two Formica picnic-style tables, ten feet apart, each running about two-hundred feet long. On the walls were jelly-stained portraits of various saints from the Middle Ages, the local bishop, some dead nuns, and President Johnson. Patrick walked over to his regular spot at the first-grade table. He sat down next to the missing-tooth kid, Jimmy Purvis. Jimmy was snarfing down a peanut butter on Wonder Bread sandwich.

"Hey, where's your lunch box?" Jimmy asked.

"I lost it." Patrick shook out his lunch bag on the table.

"What's that?" Jimmy said.

"Nothing."

"Hey! Looks like a note." Jimmy shouted. Several others overheard and looked at Patrick.

"Open it up, and see what it says," a girl yelled.

Patrick unfolded the note. It was his Mom's handwriting. Jimmy grabbed the note and read it aloud:

Dear Patrick,

I gave you the last piece of chocolate cake. Remember to say grace. And say hi to Ebby.

Love, Mom

The kids laughed. Peanut butter saliva hung down where Jimmy's tooth should have been as he hee-hawed right in Patrick's face. Then a chant broke out—repeated, first by a few, then by a crowd of more than fifty.

"Remember to say Grace, and say hi to Ebby.

Remember to say Grace, and say hi to Ebby...."

Patrick gripped his milk to slosh the whole crowd, when the top priest walked in—Monsignor Joseph Thomas Patrick O'Day. Monsignor O'Day wore a long, black cassock with red M-and-M shaped buttons running down the front. His hair was white, his eyes blue and his hands gentle like they had never reattached a greasy bicycle chain on a hot day. But they were also powerful-looking hands, ready to point at a diving, fiery airplane and maybe save it from crashing. As a young priest, O'Day had gained some fame in the Diocese by allowing a non-Catholic term life insurance salesman who had burned his sales quota pamphlets to get baptized with a group of infants. He had also heard the deathbed confessions of hourly-rate appliance repairmen and tax preparers. Gangsters, chorus girls, baseball players and politicians all knew Monsignor O'Day. He was always holding a raffle or a roast or a party to raise money for the enormous church and school building. The children were afraid of him because he once showed them a rosary that had been blessed at Fatima where the Hail Mary beads turned to gold. He walked between the rows of cafeteria tables like an apostle in a leper colony. The children got quiet. He scanned the crowd, and his lips formed the word, "Ebby?"

Patrick's teacher stood up and walked over to greet him. "Hello, Monsignor," she said, struggling to swallow the remnants of a fish rectangle.

"Hello, Sister Lucy. I've never seen a class so fervent about remembering to say Grace. But tell me, what is this 'Say hi to Ebby' that you taught them?"

"I don't know, Monsignor. I think it has something to do with one of the students whose mother is having a baby."

"Oh, well, it's good to see more Catholics being born."

"Yes, Monsignor."

Sensing no immediate danger, the children went back to eating. Monsignor and Sister Lucy, two of the oldest servants of the parish, stood visiting. Monsignor spoke in a soft, Irish mumble.

"How was your trip to the nun's convention?"

"Oh, wonderful, those waters really bubbled."

"What? *You drank bubbly?*"

Sister Lucy blushed. "Monsignor, after all these years, I still never know when you're kidding"

"Let me ask you another one," he said, "are you nuns still considering it?"

Sister Lucy looked back at the nun's table, then at Monsignor. "You mean voting to no longer wear our black habits?"

"Yes."

"Well, the Pope and the Bishop have approved it, and many of the young nuns think it might help with recruitment."

Monsignor looked at all the children and wondered how many would give up the world to become priests or nuns. "Recruitment ... Times have certainly changed. You know, when I was seventeen, I gave up a chance to wear a Cardinals baseball uniform to wear this black uniform? The scout wanted me to sign."

"Yes, I know."

"Have I told you that one already?"

"Yes, Monsignor."

"Well, I know as dear as you are, you certainly gave up a chance to wear a white dress."

She nodded.

"I should let you eat. But let me get the children's attention to tell them a story."

Sister Lucy reached in her pocket and pulled out her choir-time pitch whistle. She blew an F-sharp across the cafeteria. A feeling of dread came over the students, fearing they would be forced to sing. Sister Lucy told them to listen to Monsignor O'Day who took the floor like a Vaudeville performer.

"Hello, kids, does anyone here have a deck of cards?"

No response.

"That's okay, I have one." He pulled a poker deck from his cassock pocket. "Now, keep your eyes on the Queen of Hearts." He held up the Queen of Hearts and showed it to everyone. Then he slipped it back in the deck and shuffled it like a riverboat gambler. He raised his eyebrows, and spun around on his heels a full turn.

"C'mon, now, I need a volunteer," he said, fanning out the deck. "Somebody ... You there, pretty girl, are you Irish? Come here."

A blonde girl from third grade got up. Everyone clapped.

"What's your name?"

"Stacy Malacheski."

"Mala-*what?* Oh, go sit back down. No, I'm only kidding. That's a lovely name, and you're a lovely girl. Now pick a card, any card."

She picked one.

"Hold it up for everyone to see."

It was the Queen of Hearts. Everyone clapped.

"Thank you, Stacy, now enjoy your lunch, and be sure to obey your parents. And if you can, try to marry an Irishman."

She went to her seat.

"Let's give another round for Stacy … O'Malley," he said. Everyone clapped again. Monsignor put away the cards and gathered his thoughts. "Now kids, I want to remind you all to get out there in this, the final week before Holy Week, and sell those Cutlass Supreme raffle tickets."

He held up a fist full of freshly printed raffle booklets and fanned them like a deck of cards. "Remember, it's for a good cause, the new church air conditioning. And I'm sure God will reward you for helping."

As he ate his tuna sandwich, Patrick watched Monsignor wave raffle tickets in the air and hoped that when Monsignor left, the kids would not return to teasing him about Ebby.

"Anybody need some extra booklets to sell?" Monsignor asked the children. Nobody wanted them.

"Well, OK, I'll sell them myself. But do *try* to get out there and sell what you already have." He walked away, looking a little discouraged. He wondered if he should have begun with the yo-yo trick instead of the cards. Monsignor waved goodbye to Sister Lucy and the other nuns. Then, pausing by the cafeteria steam trays, he noticed the meat. In the old days, meat would not have been served during Lent. He breathed through the side of his mouth farthest from the meat to avoid the savory broth aroma as he headed back to the priest's house.

The chant started up again.

"Remember to say Grace, and say hi to Ebby…"

Patrick made a fist to hit someone, anyone. But before he could land a punch, Sister Lucy blew another F-sharp. Time for recess.

- chapter eight -

AT RECESS, HUNDREDS OF UNIFORMED boys and girls from grades one through four filled the playground. It was a big blacktop lot enclosed by a high chain link fence and patrolled by Mothers' Club guards. The kids knew summer was coming soon because green leaves from beyond the school property were now sprouting through the fence. Each recess was getting warmer, and the older boys smelled like B.O. Soon the nuns would have to release them from their fenced prison.

And today, the kids cheered as the janitor appeared on the flat school roof three stories up. He waved to the children and began the Annual Dropping of the Kickballs, a favorite springtime ritual.

Kids lined up beneath the school's copper gutter and waited for the winter's supply of kickballs to fall, one after another, in slow motion, their soft, maroon rubber making an oriental sound when they hit the blacktop. *K'bwoing.* After the first bounce, students chased after them. Patrick watched the figure of the janitor on the school roof, opposite the gold figure of the Virgin on the church roof. Rumor had it that Mary had once appeared to the janitor in the boiler room and that she promised to watch over Mary Queen of Our Hearts parish. Patrick squinted against the clear blue sky and studied the silhouette of the janitor. He wondered if it was true, or maybe it was just one of those things adults said to keep kids from busting windows.

Once the ritual was over and the balls had all been chased down, Patrick ran down by the church to a corner of the playground where baselines were marked by orange paint. A kickball game was starting and home plate was right next to where the priests lived in a rock house with a flat-topped garage adorned with the church's rusting air conditioner. The door to the priest house opened, and a German shepherd lurched out tugging a leash attached to Father Maligan. The dog barked at the children. Some of the kids made snarly faces and barked back.

"All right, you birds … Keep back! Keep back!" Maligan shouted.

Maligan, a red-faced priest with pins-and-needles feet, walked the dog to his black 1952 Buick. The dog jumped in, and Maligan plopped down on the driver's seat. The car rocked, and the long neck of an empty bottle rolled into view from under the seat. Maligan rubbed his knee and watched the kids running around before he shut the door and started the car. Purple smoke coughed out. Jimmy Purvis, the missing tooth kid, ran up to the car and wrote BIRD with his finger in the dust on the fender. The dog barked at Jimmy, harking dog saliva on the inside of the car window as Maligan pulled away.

It was Patrick's turn at home plate. The pitcher rolled and bounced the ball toward him and he kicked a pop fly. The second baseman, a girl with electric tape holding her black glasses together, caught it with a *whump*. He was out. He wandered over by the priest's garage. When the Mothers' Club guard wasn't looking, he ducked inside and scrambled toward the secret fort. It was only a temporary fort made of rummage sale merchandise, and after the sale all the junk would be hauled away. But until then, it was a little bit of paradise, and the kids played in it whenever they could sneak in. He climbed over some old chairs, then underneath a ping-pong table and through a tunnel of rolled-up wire fencing. Crawling on his elbows and knees, he emerged out of the other end of the tunnel into an open space. It was a small area enclosed by an upright piano, a roll top desk, and a torn pool table. Above him was an upside-down sofa and a splattered paint tarp. Weak sunlight filtered in. Patrick looked around to make sure he was alone. He picked his nose. It offered some comfort, but not much.

He got out his Knucklehead Smith wallet and looked in the money compartment. It was empty except for a booklet of unsold Cutlass Supreme raffle tickets. He shut that section and opened the photo section. There he saw his blood type identification card, which the police would have peeled from his bloody body if the train had killed him. He looked at a family photograph. John's hair was getting longer since the Beatles had released their latest album. Then he flipped the wallet to the secret picture he had of Ebby. He relaxed and leaned against the piano. He took it out of the plastic. It was from the day the school portraits were handed out. Patrick had thrown all the other girl's pictures in the trash. But Ebby's, he kept. He studied her smile and her brown eyes and black hair. He pressed his lips to the photo, and all his concerns about almost getting smashed by freight trains, the janitor seeing the Virgin in the boiler room, and his unsold Cutlass Supreme tickets melted away. He closed his eyes and felt the warm glow of the new thing wash over him.

Then, his eyes flashed open as he heard something move. It sounded like a small animal. Something was coming. He wiped the lip marks off Ebby's picture and stuffed it in his wallet. Jimmy Purvis crawled out of the rolled up fence tunnel.

"Patrick, I wondered where you were! You're up."

"I don't want to play anymore."

"We need you. The other team has a new player."

"Who?"

"Ebby."

Patrick crawled through the fence tunnel like a dog after a squirrel. Jimmy followed him, yelling details down the tunnel. "She was only out this morning because her mom was having a baby, and she was up all night. She asked for you … She asked, 'Where's Patrick?'"

Patrick ran out of the garage and immediately to the plate. The pitcher wound up. Patrick could see Ebby out in the center field. She waved to him. "It's a girl," she yelled. The pitcher rolled the ball. It bounced on the asphalt. Patrick kicked it high and clean, launching it toward the outfield. Ebby caught it, her skinny arms clutching it to her chest as Patrick's heart flip-flopped.

"Out!" someone yelled.

"We win!" some boys on Ebby's team hollered.

Sister Lucy blew another F-sharp and recess was over. But Ebby looked right at him and smiled from the outfield. Did she feel the new thing for him, too? Patrick had never been happier.

- chapter nine -

AS SOON AS HE GOT HOME, Patrick decided to celebrate with an ice-cold glass of Vess orange soda. He pulled out a family-sized bottle from the pantry, scrounged in the drawer for the bottle opener, and popped the top. But when the fizz whooshed out, and the cap danced on the countertop, he heard his mom's fast-approaching footsteps.

"What are you doing?" Mom said, coming around the corner, "It's Lent."

He picked up the bottle cap and tried to press it back on, but once it was opened it couldn't be resealed to keep from going flat. "I'm sorry," Patrick said, I forgot."

"*You forgot?* Did Jesus forget and drink orange soda in the desert when he was tempted?"

"I don't know, I guess not," he said looking at the floor. He felt bad about it, but he was still thirsty.

"That's right. He remembered. But you ... Have you even sold any raffle tickets for the church?"

He put down the bottle and admitted he hadn't sold a single one.

"Patrick, you have to get going," she said gently, "It's almost Easter."

So, he abandoned his orange soda, took his Cutlass Supreme tickets from his wallet, and trudged out the front door and into the world alone. He went next door first, but nobody was home. Then he went to the next house and banged the doorknocker. A dog yapped wildly and a lady in corpse-white facial cream opened the door and peered at him through the screen. She held a poodle as it barked and squirmed and bared its sharp brown teeth. The lady hushed the dog, told Patrick to come back after Easter, and then closed the door right in his face.

Farther down the street, he saw the Lutheran man who never smiled out working in his garden. As Patrick approached, the man straightened up and held out his hand.

"You see this worm?" the man said, handing a red wiggler to Patrick. "Someday they'll eat us all."

Patrick took the worm and pretended to examine it. "That's some worm," he said and handed the worm back with the packet of Cutlass Supreme tickets. But the Lutheran man wasn't buying anything Catholic. He handed the tickets back to Patrick with worm marks all over them, and then he tossed the worm back in the mud. Patrick was almost ready to give up when he headed down by the creek where the old German couple lived. At least they were Catholic.

Herb Metzenhoffer was cutting his yard in precise strips with his electric mower, taking care to keep the cord away from the blade. A retired accountant, Metzenhoffer was thin, quick, and thrifty. He had carried a bag lunch to work for years and even re-used the bags. At night, neighbors could tell which room he was in because Metzenhoffer turned off the light when he left one room and turned on a new light when he entered another. When he cut the yard, Metzenhoffer kept his handkerchief at the ready, periodically dabbing his forehead. He moved across the grass as if he had a busy schedule packed with important places to go. Patrick ran across the lawn flashing the packet of Cutlass tickets. But Metzenhoffer shook his head no, kept on cutting, and muttered something sternly in German.

Speeding around the side of the house, Patrick could see Octavia Metzenhoffer standing by the creek. A white-haired woman, she was wearing a faded flowery dress and yellow rubber gloves. Her back was turned, so she couldn't see Patrick. He slowed down and watched as she tossed handfuls of white powder from a bag into the creek. Patrick stuffed his tickets in his pocket, and began to pretend that if he could sneak up on her, Mrs. Metzenhoffer would turn into Ebby, and they would dance together. He stalked slowly along the edge of the creek like the Wolfman. A channel of sewer water trickled over the rocks. He was almost behind her.

"Gross, what stinks?" he blurted out.

Mrs. Metzenhoffer, who had been humming a German harvest song from her youth, spun around, surprised, and dropped the bag on her foot. A poof of powdered lye shot up her dress.

"Mein Gott, pass auf, Patrick!" she said. Mrs. Metzenhoffer put her hand on Patrick's shoulder. She studied him and wondered what it would have been like to have children when the lye penetrated her thigh pores and began to itch. She couldn't contain herself, but she couldn't scratch right there in the yard, either. So to circulate air up her dress, she started dancing the harvest polka. Patrick reached out his hands and danced with her.

They danced around the honeysuckled back yard in a pattern that had been in Mrs. Metzenhoffer's family since her great-grandparents had met during the 1883 wheat harvest. Patrick didn't know any of the footwork, but his Keds hopped along well enough. They danced and danced until they ended up back over by the edge of the creek. Then the smell hit Patrick again.

"What smells?" he said dancing.

"Death," she said spinning around. "It's the smell of death ... a dead opossum."

They got near the edge again, and Patrick could see the dead opossum under the lye powder. It had a pink snout, glassy eyes and claws reaching out, frozen stiff in death. Flies buzzed over the corpse.

"Why did it die?" he said.

"Everything dies," she said.

Just then, a big City of Webster Groves dump truck screeched to a halt in front of the Metzenhoffer's house. The lawn mower stopped. Two truck doors slammed. Mr. Metzenhoffer and two city workers marched around the back. Mr. Metzenhoffer saw his wife dancing.

"Octavia! This isn't Oktoberfest. The city men are here."

She hurried inside to wash her legs. The city workers, a heavy-set black man and a skinny white man with a smoker's cough, climbed down into the creek. The dead smell grabbed them.

"Shit," the fat man said.

"Shit," the skinny one said.

Patrick remembered seeing the word on the bridge. It apparently had something to do with creeks and bridges. The fat one scooped up the dead opossum with a shovel. The skinny one held open a plastic bag at arm's length and turned his head to cough.

"This is quite a change of scenery," the skinny one said, "We was playing a game of hearts with the lady *dis*-patcher when you called. They got this new lady *dis*-patcher. Boy is she—"

"Make sure for the maggots, too," Metzenhoffer interrupted.

Mr. Metzenhoffer dabbed his forehead with his handkerchief as he supervised the clean-up. The fat one shoveled up some squirming maggots and dropped them in the bag. The skinny worker spun the bag shut and knotted it. Patrick and Mr. Metzenhoffer watched the city workers struggle to climb out of the creek. They slipped and cursed and got all muddy, then they were out.

"Shit," the fat one said, brushing the mud off his pants and hoping for a tip. "That was a real nasty job ... Yes siree." He wiped his forehead with his arm and looked to see if Mr. Metzenhoffer was reaching for his wallet. Metzenhoffer stood stock still with his hands on his hips. Unhappy with his ever-rising property taxes, Metzenhoffer was hoping they would offer to take his yard clippings for free.

Patrick sensed an opportunity. He reached into his pocket. "Would anyone be interested in a Cutlass Supreme raffle ticket?"

The adults all looked at him and said nothing. The skinny city worker took the raffle packet and read it. "I never have no luck," he said. He handed it to the fat one. "You want one?"

The fat one read the top ticket. "A dollar, huh? Sorry, but my Budweiser money is low enough." He handed the packet to Metzenhoffer.

"I'll walk you out front," Metzenhoffer said, "I've been cutting the lawn. I've got a small pile of clippings."

The city workers walked past Metzenhoffer's grass clippings and threw the dead opossum in the back of the dump truck. His thin lips pursed, Metzenhoffer stood by his pile and watched them pull away. The city workers waved and smiled, but by the time the truck was in second gear, they were cursing the old man for not tipping. Metzenhoffer handed the raffle packet back to Patrick.

"Well, how about it?" Patrick said.

"How about what?"

"You want one?"

"We already have a new car," Metzenhoffer said, pointing to his 1948 Buick in the garage.

Hot and discouraged, Patrick went home. Mom was downstairs in the basement doing laundry, so he popped a couple of chunks of ice out of the frosty ice tray and dropped them into an aluminum cup. He put his fingers over them to stop them from rattling and then filled the cup with orange soda and sneaked out behind the garage to think about it all. He sat down and leaned against the garage. After a few deep, refreshing slurps, he picked up a stick and started drawing in the mud. It reminded him of a story in the Bible when Jesus drew something in the mud. Patrick always wondered *what* Jesus drew, because no one ever talked about it. That was the problem with church. They left out the good parts and had too many boring parts. Maybe it was a horse, or sunset, or a secret formula only Jesus knew, and he had to erase it before a spy could spot it and tell everybody. After a few minutes, Patrick set the stick aside and admired his work. *E-b-b-y.*

- chapter ten -

ON EASTER MORNING, THE CANTWELL'S 1959 Falcon raced down Main Street under the train bridge. They were late for Mass again. Dad zoomed to a stop on the school playground, which was already packed with parked cars. They got out and moved fast. A church song was humming through the stained glass windows, as their dress shoes quick-stepped across the pavement.

Patrick adjusted his clip-on tie and examined his conscience. He had disobeyed his Dad and gone on the train tracks, jumped in front of a train, lied, sneaked orange soda, and failed to sell enough raffle tickets. He looked at the old church air conditioner, rusting away on top of the garage, and the gold statue of Mary on the roof watching over the parish. The only raffle tickets he had sold were one to Dad and one to Granddad Cantwell. Eight more were still tucked in his wallet, unsold.

They all slinked in the back door, dipped their hands in the holy water, and made signs of the cross while the organ was laboring and the crowd was singing "Oh, Holy, Holy." An usher who looked like Al Capone in a blue pinstriped suit with two-toned shoes gave Dad the nod and told him there was no room, except for scattered seats in the balcony and maybe three seats together way up front by the altar.

Dad leaned toward the usher and whispered. "Listen, I wonder if I could ask you a favor … Have you got any seats in back?"

The usher stepped back and blanched. "This isn't the Muny Opera. The front seats go last."

Dad looked at Patrick and John. "Boys, it looks like you'll have to go up in

Kevin Killeen

the balcony. But *be good* ... I don't want to see you hanging over the railing. Sit in the back up there where it's safe."

The usher led Mom and Dad and Teddy up the center aisle. Dad walked quickly. He thought of the eyes on him, Catholic eyes that had gone to Catholic schools and Masses all their lives. He had only gone to public schools, but he had always attended Mass with his mother, and he wanted to raise a good Catholic family. He really did. But he always felt like an outsider at Mary Queen of Our Hearts. To him the Progressive Dinner, Dixieland Night, the Mission Carnival—all events Mom loved—were excruciating exercises in hand-shaking and self-promoting small talk. *Why the hell should I get involved with these people? I don't sell insurance,"* he had protested before one Progressive Dinner. Dad had been the bottom bunk under five sailors on the Battleship Missouri, and, to him, the parish was just another battleship full of draftees and superiors, busy work and marching orders. It wasn't a place to advance socially or be noticed. It was just a place to serve your time and hope for an honorable discharge.

But now, his boys had put him right square in the public eye. Because they couldn't drag themselves out of bed or away from watching *Johnny Quest*, because they had eaten piles of pancakes in their underwear instead of getting dressed and brushing their teeth when their mom told them to, he had to tiptoe down the center aisle with everyone watching. Losing shoes, taking too long with the funny papers, or spending too much time in front of the mirror like Mom, his family was always making him late for Mass. He'd have preferred to stay home rather than provide a Cantwell parade for the whole parish's entertainment.

The usher nodded toward the front pew. Everyone looked at Dad. He genuflected and kneeled to say a quick Our Father. Teddy sat in the pew beside him and looked around for Mom.

Mom was walking slowly up the center aisle. She took each step in time with the song, like a bride keeping the beat with the bridal march. "Oh, Holy, Holy," she sang as parishioners turned in their pews the way customers used to swivel on stools at the Parkmoor. Her Bridge Club friends, knowing she was pregnant again, nodded and smiled. To Mom, it was an honor to be late, an honor to walk down the aisle to the best seat in the house.

Patrick and John clambered up the back steps to the balcony. If they had to be at church, they'd at least get to enjoy a scenic bluff without parental supervision. They pushed and maneuvered, and finally were able to squeeze between a couple of other worshipers for prime seats on the front row. They

42

leaned over the railing and took in the view. Some people kneeled. Some older men and women half-kneeled, resting their bottoms on the pews. An ocean of Easter hats with yellow and pink flowers and white nets rolled gently like sea foam on wave crests as women shifted in their pews. Men's bald spots reflected overhead lights. Bright sunlight streaked in through stained-glass windows and cast glittering jewel-colored speckles on marble saint statues and gold altar decorations.

Wearing a long, purple robe trimmed with white lace and a gold rope belt, Monsignor O'Day glided from one side of the altar to the other, reminding Patrick of some powerful alien from a recent episode of *Lost in Space*. Monsignor read the story of the empty tomb, then kissed the big red book and closed it. He leaned forward on the podium and looked out at his flock. Every pew was packed. The balcony was full. Twice-a-year Catholics leaned along the back walls. People coughed. This would be his biggest sermon of the year. He paused briefly, waiting for a sermon to occur.

Never one to over plan, Monsignor O'Day created sermons like dreams. They were honest, spontaneous compilations of recent images and life-long concerns stitched together by sudden transitions. No one knew what he might say, not even Monsignor O'Day. It was this style that gave his sermons a lively, Vaudeville quality. His Mass was always the most popular and was often quoted at Bridge Club. He cleared his throat, and decided to dive in.

"Easter is my favorite holiday. It's more important even than the other big one ... St. Patrick's Day."

Patrick's mind wandered as he looked around the church. He spotted Jimmy Purvis. Jimmy sat in the aisle seat of a pew with his parents, and Patrick could see he was secretly unwrapping a purple foil chocolate egg. The egg jostled in his grip. It slipped into the aisle and rolled in loopy circles. Everyone saw it. Jimmy's father, an abrasive chemical salesman, cracked him on the back of the neck. Then Al Capone rushed to avert a crisis, genuflected, grabbed the egg, and retreated to the back. Patrick looked around for something else to look at. Monsignor continued.

"The year was 1926. Pennant fever. A scout saw me playing in a sandlot and asked me, 'How'd you like to play ball for the Redbirds?'"

Patrick looked around some more. The stained glass windows and the statues were old stuff to him. He needed something fresh, something new and interesting. Then he saw it—up above the altar by the fireproof ceiling tile. It was a marble figure of a gargoyle. Like a Wolfman with wings. He had never noticed it before. You had to be in the balcony to see it at eye level. It was solid, but in the jittery, stained-glass light, it seemed alive and ready to pounce.

He looked below it. There was a girl in a pink hat with black hair.

Ebby.

Ebby and her family were in mortal danger. They were seated almost directly beneath the grotesque creature. Any moment now, it might stretch out its wings, zing around the church a time or two, and then dive down to peck out Ebby's eyeballs. Her older brother Raven, the one who had told her to jump in front of a train, didn't even care. He was just sitting there with his black hair, ripping a page of the hymnal book into little pieces that fell on the floor. Patrick formulated a plan of action. He would protect Ebby and her family, and, while saving the day, he would make up for his poor sales of Cutlass Supreme tickets. Monsignor waved his hands in the air.

"And now, the nuns want to trade in their habits for bell bottoms. *Recruitment!* I see a pattern. First the young people start singing 'Kumbaya'…."

Patrick leaned over the balcony, aimed his crossbow and fired an arrow attached to a rope. It shot over the crowd and stuck with a *pfump* in the fireproof ceiling tile above the gargoyle. John grabbed the loose end and knotted the rope securely around the legs of Mrs. Fernbacher's pipe organ bench. A cake-loving woman, she provided a secure anchor. Patrick eased out over the railing, grabbed the rope, and began the dangling, hand-over-hand journey above the crowd toward the stone-faced gargoyle.

"Then they took away our Latin Mass, and made us speak English. I understand there's even a plan to have everyone shake hands and say 'peace' to each other. *Peace?* I'm sure some men are hoping to sit next to a dizzy blonde…."

The gargoyle's eyes snapped opened.

Blink.

They were dark and glassy. The creature took a breath. Its marble chest filled with air, and it's cold, carved scales softened to scabby flesh. Hair grew. Feathers lengthened. It moved. It turned its head and looked directly at Patrick. It looked down at Ebby. None of the parishioners saw it, none were aware of the danger—except an infant with colic in pew sixteen. The baby boy screamed. His mother hefted him to her shoulder and clopped down the aisle toward the cry room. Monsignor continued.

"What happened to the Catholic tradition of working, struggling, striving to make our souls worthy to go to heaven?" Monsignor asked, his eyes scanning the room for reaction.

Swipe. Swipe. It clawed out for Patrick, but came up short. It scooted closer. Then its claws hit the rope. *Kthonggggggg*. The arrow loosened. Bits of fireproof ceiling tile tinkled on the altar like flecks of snow. The gargoyle looked down at Ebby and licked its lips, the rope slackened, and Patrick tumbled down toward a cluster of bald spots.

"Careful!" John hissed, grabbing the back of Patrick's sports coat as he leaned a bit too far over the choir loft railing.

Monsignor O'Day looked up at the disturbance. "That's right. Let's be careful today as we go about our activities. Thank you for supporting the raffle. We came just short of our target. But we'll start on the new air conditioner someday. God bless you all and Happy Easter. And remember this, as you sit down to your meals, remember to say Grace and say hi … to everyone."

Mrs. Fernbacher leaned into the pipe organ and blew out some real heavy chords. Sinking back into the pew, Patrick and John watched her bare feet tapping across the base note pedals. Her black shoes sat waiting nearby.

- chapter eleven -

EBBY'S FAMILY LEFT through the side door. Patrick hurried down the balcony steps so he could loop around and see her, but Dad stopped Patrick, then John at the bottom of the steps. "Let's all stick together. Your mother wants to take a picture."

That very instant, Granddad Cantwell, who had bought only one raffle ticket—just to be nice—pulled up in front of the church in his new Cutlass Supreme. Smoking a two-dollar cigar, he enjoyed each puff as it twisted in the flow of air conditioning and slipped out the window. Beside him, his wife of forty-one years, Nana Cantwell, sat holding a handkerchief to her nose. She looked out the window at the people posing for pictures as they poured out of church.

"There they are," Nana said.

Granddad blasted the horn.

Jimmy Purvis's father looked down the hill in front of the church. He saw the car, and shouted the news. "Look, everybody, it's the Cutlass!"

Heads turned. Small talk stopped. A crowd of hundreds began running across the grass toward the Cutlass. Bonnets blew off. An old man slipped in the dewy grass. Children trampled him. A woman's high heel punched a hole in the sod. The mud sucked her shoe off. She kept running. Patrick's parents looked more carefully from the church steps. "*Why, look,* down by that car. *It's your father,*" Mom said.

"Pop?" Dad said to himself.

Dad started running toward the car. Had his Pop really won the Cutlass?

This was an Easter miracle. Patrick and John sprinted ahead. Mom grabbed Teddy's hand and followed at a pregnant jog. The mob rushed closer, vaulting over the first barricade of Vatican bushes. The usher who looked like Al Capone stumbled and crashed through the plywood "He Has Risen" promotional sign. He rose up and kept running. Granddad Cantwell got out of the car and strained to see what everyone was running from.

"Must be an egg hunt," he mumbled. The crowd ran directly to the car. Nana locked her door. They pressed their faces against the passenger side window with the price sticker. The mob petted and pushed and rocked the car on its shock absorbers.

Granddad Cantwell yelled with nicotine-rich blood rising in his face, *"Get back! Don't touch it! This is private property!"*

Patrick broke through the crowd. "Granddad," he yelled jumping up and down. "You won! I sold you the winning ticket!"

"What?" He turned to the crowd. "You people think I won this? This isn't the raffle car. *I bought this car with my own money. Paid cash!"*

The crowd fell silent. Shoulders slumped. Jimmy Purvis's father was the first to regain perspective. He shouted the good news. "Hey, everybody, this means we all still have a chance! C'mon, let's find out when the drawing will be." He led his son, dressed in a matching green plaid sports jacket, back up the hill. The crowd turned back.

Dad shook hands with Granddad.

"What do you think?" Granddad said, turning to the car.

"Pop, you've caused a sensation here today … the church, the boys."

Granddad took his cigar from his mouth. "I'm sorry, but I didn't cause it," he winked at the boys. "Life *is* a sensation. And then the sensation stops."

Patrick and John hugged Granddad. They didn't understand that he had once been a boy just like them. To them, he had always been old, and they would always be young. He patted their heads with his veiny hands.

"You boys hungry?"

"Yeah."

"Well, we're going to eat some of the finest fried chicken you'll ever eat in your whole life," he said. "And that's not all. We've got presents." He smiled at them. His teeth were yellow from age and cigars, but he had a giving smile. Standing there in the waxed reflection of the Cutlass and the realization that the Mass was really over and fried chicken and presents lay ahead, the boys were happy. Then the church bell rang the half hour. Mom looked back at the church roof with the statue of Mary and then at her watch. It was 11:30.

"Don't forget, we have to stop by the cloister and pick up Sister Jenny," Mom said.

"Do they let her out?" Nana asked. "I thought it was against the rules."

"She can still leave on family visits during this trial year," Mom said.

"I admire her, what she's doing," Nana said.

Mom nodded, trying to be proud of her sister.

"How's the food they serve them?" Granddad asked. "Is it any good?"

"I don't know. But she'll be hungry today. She's been on a fast."

"Good gravy, the poor girl," Granddad said.

Patrick and John rode with Nana and Granddad in the brand new Cutlass. Teddy cried a little when he saw he couldn't go with his big brothers. Life for him was all about wondering what he was missing. But then he remembered that sometimes it was good to have Mom and Dad all to himself. Teddy climbed in the back seat of the Falcon, a small sedan, which the boys called "the headache car," because its upholstery smelled like an old man's sports coat and gave them headaches. Dad pulled out in front of the Cutlass and looked in the rear view mirror at the gleaming grillwork. Through the windshield, he could see his Pop smiling.

"So, he went and bought it. That's really something. I hope he isn't overdoing it with the boys," Dad said.

Granddad lined up the air conditioner vents to blow into the back seat as he puffed his cigar.

"Feel that modern, fresh air, boys," he said. The cigar smoke blew into the back seat. Eager to press buttons, Granddad turned on the radio past some preachers and static to the Music of Your Life station. The song "Winchester Cathedral" was playing. It was a jaunty tune about a groom left behind at the altar.

Driving down Main Street through Webster Groves, pink, yellow and white buds were shaking on the trees like admirers throwing confetti along Lindbergh's parade route. Granddad took a deep breath. "Boys, look around and remember this beautiful, brief day. We're all alive … and we're all together."

He took the cigar from his mouth, and rolled down the window all the way. Making sure no cars were passing, he took a deep breath and summoned up his complete inventory of morning phlegm. He leaned his head into the breeze and spit. It flashed in the sunlight and fell on the pavement.

"Gone forever," he said.

"*Joe!* Your manners!" Nana said. "*The boys!*"

"Oh, sorry." He looked in his rear view mirror at the boys, then back at his wife. "Well, they're old enough to spit."

They slipped under the train bridge as a silver passenger train with people eating ham brunch shot overhead. In the Falcon, Teddy was standing on the back seat looking out the rear view window at the train and the Cutlass.

"Be careful, Teddy, sit down," Dad said, "You might get killed if we have an accident."

"Oh, he'll be all right, it's Easter," Mom said, reaching around to pat Teddy's back. "Nothing bad can happen on Easter. I just hope everything goes well."

Dad checked the gas gauge. The tank was full. "What do you mean?"

"I don't know. I just wonder how to tell her *the news.*"

"The news?" Dad said.

"*That I'm pregnant again,*" she said.

"Oh, that. Hmmm," Dad said, but he was already thinking about something else. "Look," he began, "when we get to the restaurant, I want to get the check."

"Wait a minute … what about what *I* said? How am I going to tell my sister—"

"What's there to tell?" Dad said, raising his voice. "Just say, I'm pregnant, pass the chicken."

"You're not funny." Mom gritted her teeth at him.

"I'm not trying to be," Dad said. He took his eyes off the road and stared at her. "I'm thirty-nine years old and Pop never lets me get the check."

"He can afford it. But don't you see? I'm afraid my sister can't afford … *the idea* that I'm having all these babies, and she's going to be an old nun in the cloister someday without a family."

Dad gripped the steering wheel. "How much is in the checking account?"

"Oh, I don't know," she said looking out the window.

"Well, what *do* you know?" Dad snapped.

"I don't know how to tell her."

"Well, don't ask me. I'm under a lot of pressure downtown. I can't think like a nun."

"She's not a nun yet!" Mom said slapping the dashboard.

"What?" Dad's eyes were wide.

"I mean, she's really only *half* nun," Mom said softly. "I know it's wrong, but sometimes I wish she would drop out, go back to college and get married someday," Mom said. "I always thought we would have families together."

"Look, I think I should get that check today. How much is in the checking account?"

"I don't know."

Teddy was sitting in the back seat watching the argument as the car bounced along and the sunlight warmed the Falcon upholstery. He tapped his Dad on the shoulder. They stopped fighting and looked at Teddy.

"Can we get a new car like Granddad? I'm getting a headache."

- chapter twelve -

THE CANTWELL CARS pulled off the main road into the heavily wooded compound of the cloistered nunnery. At the guard booth, a nun with dark sunglasses and a walkie-talkie checked Dad's driver's license, then wrote something on a clipboard and opened the gate. Obeying the ten-mile-an-hour speed limit, Dad curled the Falcon down the driveway past a meadow where nuns in white habits walked alone on a prayer path. Granddad Cantwell, glancing at his watch, considered making a daring pass, one that would sling gravel, but he looked at Nana, who shook her head against the idea, so he held back.

They came to a stop in front of a white stone building, across from a pond with lily pads and ducks. In the center of the pond stood a concrete angel. The warning angel held one finger to its lips reminding visitors to keep quiet, and the other pointed toward heaven. Granddad revved his engine to blast out any carbon deposits that may have formed in the past few miles. Ducks took flight, dripping water as they flapped away.

"When do we get our presents?" shouted Teddy from the Falcon window toward Granddad's car.

Granddad smiled and shouted back. "They're in the trunk. How about right now?"

"*Not now, Joe,*" whispered Nana, "We don't want to cause another sensation. *Not here at the cloister.*"

Dad got out of the Falcon. He nodded cautious hellos to passing nuns, as he walked with Mom and Teddy up to the smoking Cutlass. The nuns prayed for them.

Dad leaned down to Granddad's open window and whispered. "Pop, maybe you could rest your engine. We've got to go get Sister Jenny inside."

"But, look at the time. *Our reservation's for noon.* Maybe she's waiting in the front hallway, you know, just putting on some final lipstick." He honked his horn for her. A magnificent, trumpet note leaped from the car's grillwork and soared across the fields and prayer paths. Startled nuns jumped.

"Pop, they don't wear lipstick."

"Joe, turn *off* the car!" Nana shot him one of her looks.

Granddad cut the engine. Mom took Dad's hand to take him into the cloister with her, but Dad eyed the ivy-covered archway and sensed he didn't belong. He wriggled his fingers free.

"Patrick, go inside with your mother."

"Dad, I want to stay outside. Our presents…."

"Patrick, be good."

Granddad opened the door to let Patrick out. Looking around, Granddad viewed the virgin property and estimated its value on the commercial real estate market. It seemed ideal for a factory, subdivision, or golf course. He puffed his cigar. But it had lost its vigor. He lobbed it toward an open trashcan by the door. It was a hole in one.

Patrick and Mom walked up the steps to the cloister. They were uneven stone steps, pocked from 115 years of rain and repentance. He could hear his brother John tearing gift-wrap behind him.

"*A guitar!*" John shouted, and began strumming.

Inside the front hallway, Patrick and Mom paused to get used to the dark. The air smelled of candle wax and Mr. Clean. They walked slowly down a stone corridor, lit only by stained glass windows recessed along the walls ten feet apart. The windows showed famous female saints and martyrs.

"She said in her letter to meet her in the chapel in the back pew," Mom whispered.

Mom's high heels clicked as they ascended the stone steps. Above them was an old nun scrubbing the landing with Mr. Clean. Surprised by the visitors, the nun dropped her scrub brush and it fell down the steps, end over end like a wet Slinky. Patrick grabbed the sudsy bristles and walked up to her. She took it from him, smiled back with dark holes where teeth used to reside, and went back to work.

They made a left and pulled open the tall wooden door into the dimly lit chapel. The clock tower began to gong the noon bells. In front of them, a dozen oak pews rippled up toward an altar flickering with candles. The flames burned in blue and red glass jars. Each struggling flame represented prayers for someone in this life or the next. It was a chapel where generations of nuns had fasted and prayed and worked in silence to tip the scales for the souls of others.

Sister Jenny was kneeling in her white habit in the front of the chapel. She was twenty-two years old now. Sister Jenny had been in the order almost a year, having joined after her father's death. She looked over her shoulder, then made the sign of the cross and got up. Patrick put his fingers in his ears. The bells tolled. He watched his aunt walk toward them. Here was the aunt whose picture was always watching him in the front hallway at home. She wore a baggy habit, and her bright green eyes looked tired, but hopeful of something just out of reach. She had a beauty that was thin and sad.

The two sisters, who had once been childhood roommates, kissed cheeks and hugged for two rings of the bell. Sister Jenny looked at Patrick. She seemed like she wanted to hug him, so he quickly stuck his arm out straight to shake hands with her from a distance. It was his general policy to never hug a nun.

"Daddy would have been so proud of you," Mom said to Sister Jenny.

Sister Jenny looked down awkwardly and patted Patrick on the head. The twelfth toll sounded, and she opened her mouth to speak her first words in forty days.

"I need to change," she whispered.

They followed her in silence down a back staircase to a hallway by the nun's common dining room. There the silence was broken by the sound of nuns talking. Sixty-six nuns, mostly older, sat around a long wooden table to eat their Easter lunch. They filled the air with chirpy, high-pitched bursts like a cage of parakeets. They sipped red cream soda from wine glasses and waited for their feast to be served. Electric blenders struggled nearby in the kitchen to pre-chew large chunks of ham for the toothless. Sister Jenny popped in the doorway and introduced her relatives to her co-workers.

"Excuse me, sisters, this is my sister, Mary Cantwell, and her son, Patrick."

The nuns stopped talking. They leaned forward or looked over their shoulders to examine her carefree green dress, her matching shoes, shiny plastic jewelry and bright spring-yellow purse. Then they looked at Patrick's Easter clothes and his haircut. The room quieted as they took in this rare fashion update from beyond their walls.

"Happy Easter," Mom blurted out. She rose up on her toes with an optimism bred from her secret pregnancy, her family, their Victorian house, her Bridge Club friends, the air-conditioned grocery store nearby, Famous Barr department store sales, James Bond novels, Frank Sinatra records and summer vacations to the beach—her whole life happily, thankfully, waiting for her outside.

"Happy Easter," the nuns said back flatly.

"Well, if you'll please excuse me, I'm going to change before we ... go," Sister Jenny said. She bowed and withdrew.

The nuns got quiet. It was a powerful word—*go*. They tapped fingernails on their empty plates and rearranged silverware at the thought of going. Patrick and Mom stood by the door. She got a comb from her purse to re-comb his hair. She tugged at his hair and tried to start a conversation with the nuns. "I just combed him an hour ago. *But you know boys.* We just came from Mass ... Mary Queen of Our Hearts. Any of you know Monsignor O'Day?" The nuns looked at each other. Nobody knew him.

Suddenly, the kitchen door swung open and hot dishes floated out on the fat arms of kitchen nuns. Heaping plates of ham, small potatoes, peas, fresh baked bread, coleslaw, cherry Jell-O and dietary pudding spun onto the table. For many of the nuns it was the end of days of fasting. They roared through Grace and began passing the plates like Frisbees.

"Don't get sick. Remember to eat slowly after your fast," an old nun with an eye patch warned. She did not serve herself yet, but looked at Patrick without smiling and beckoned him to come closer. He left Mom's side and approached the old nun.

"Yes, Ma'am."

"How old are you?" she said moving her eye up and down his suit, through his hair, down to his necktie, into his pupils. She stared deep into his soul and saw the hidden things in his life—Ebby, the tracks, the speeding freight train, the word SHIT, the Wolfman, his unsold raffle tickets.

"Seven."

She raised her wine glass of cream soda to his lips. The bubbles bit his tongue. It was his first honest sip of soda since Lent. He drank it. She studied him. To avoid her eye, he looked over her shoulder at a portrait of Bishop Borgensmoggen who resembled Boris Karloff. She took the glass from his mouth and rested it on the wooden table.

"We need priests," she told him.

All the nuns stopped chewing and looked at Patrick and the eye-patched nun.

"What are you going to be when you grow up?" she persisted.

Patrick looked in her eye. But it was too keen, too knowing, so he looked away, toward the portrait, and swallowed.

"A bishop?" he said.

The nuns all clapped, raised their wine glasses full of cream soda, and made a toast to "the future bishop." Sister Jenny appeared at the door. The old nun with the eye patch straightened Patrick's tie and told him sternly, "I'll be dead soon. But I'll pray for you. And I hope to see you in heaven someday, in the bishop section."

+ + + +

Granddad Cantwell smiled as the cold mud squished between his toes. He was barefoot with his pant legs rolled up, wading in the contemplative pond. His mission was to retrieve the tin, wind-up boat he had given as an Easter present to Teddy. On its maiden voyage, the pleasure craft had skimmed over lily pads before getting caught in the algae clinging to the base of the concrete angel. Dad held Teddy and kept a lookout for nuns. Nana was shaking her head in the passenger seat and flipping through a *National Enquirer* magazine she had bought at Straub's when no one was looking. There was an important article on Elizabeth Taylor in there somewhere. John sat on the bumper of the Cutlass, fingering his first powerful "G" chord.

"I've got it," Granddad called out. He wound up the boat and sent it back toward the family. Patrick, Mom and Sister Jenny came out the front door of the cloister. Granddad waved to them and shouted, "Ship ahoy."

They all greeted Sister Jenny and watched Granddad climb out of the pond and put his socks and shoes back on. The two Cantwell cars pulled away from the cloister and headed for the restaurant. Their Easter lunch would soon be served. Granddad patted his pocket to make sure he had another cigar for later.

Back by the entrance to the nunnery, flames leapt from the trashcan where Granddad had tossed his last cigar. The stone angel in the pond watched passively as the fire sent sparks into the parking lot and smoke up toward the heavens until a pair of nuns happened by and one of them ran and got a fire extinguisher and put it out.

- chapter thirteen -

THE TWO LOVEBIRDS was a fried chicken paradise in a red brick mansion that sat on a bluff above the Missouri Pacific train tracks. On the front lawn, a crab apple tree shaded a stone walkway that led across thick bluegrass. Tulips, red and yellow, swayed in rows around the entranceway. It was a family restaurant whose two busiest days of the year were Mother's Day and Easter. Every living, cooking mother who entered there was happy and relaxed, knowing there would be no sink full of dishes at the end of the feast.

With a slight headache, Sister Jenny stepped out of the Falcon and into the world for which she had been suffering. She watched two girls wearing pretty dresses and talking with their hands as they walked in front of two college-aged men. They were about her age. She thought of her years at Fontbonne College, where she was undeclared when she met a Washington University medical student who was not a Catholic. He made her laugh and they became friends. They went swimming and dancing. He let her drive his car, with him in the passenger seat, to practice for her driving test. Then one day on an entrance ramp, he told her he loved her, and she almost crashed into a guardrail. They laughed and she told him she loved him, too. They were happy without trying to be, and at the end of each day when she looked in the mirror, she saw a beautiful young woman smiling back at her. Then her father had the stroke.

At the hospital, alone by his bedside, she promised him things and promised God things if he would get better. Unable to speak or show any sign of hearing, he lay there, unresponsive. Then she vowed she would only marry a Catholic, and that's when she noticed Father Gottenheim in the doorway. He was an old man, thin with sunken cheeks and hunched shoulders. He smelled of last rites.

After the funeral, Gottenheim started visiting Jenny. He took her to the cemetery and to the Parkmoor for coffee. He gave her driving lessons and practiced his sermons on her as she drove. With his soft, shepherding voice, he suggested she might consider a different road. They turned into the cloister where she saw the pond and the nuns and the candles lit for the dead. Secretly, at first, she began to think about becoming a nun. The idea grew stronger while she sat at home in a corner watching the phone ring over and over. She knew it was her boyfriend. The boy she loved, but who was not a Catholic. She didn't answer it. She pulled down the shades, locked the door and drew inward. She kept a picture of her father by her bed and wondered at night, when she stared at his eyes, where his soul was and what, if anything, she could do to help him.

Sister Jenny's white habit dragged along the blacktop as she walked with Nana, Mom and Teddy. Mom thought about telling her right there that she was pregnant.

"I hope you're glad you came," Mom said to Jenny.

"I just feel a little weak," she said.

"It's that Falcon upholstery," Mom said.

"I hope they have some pretty dresses to show. The owner's wife is a real clotheshorse, and she makes all her own dresses, you know," Nana said.

The boys ran ahead to play on the rope swing hanging from the crab apple tree.

Dad and Granddad walked together.

"Pop, there's something I wanted to bring up, before we get inside," Dad said.

Granddad pulled out a handkerchief to blow his nose and a penny fell out. It rolled down the parking lot. Dad resisted the urge to go after it.

"Everything okay downtown?" Granddad said.

"Fine. Good opportunities ahead."

Granddad blew his nose. "You've got a lot on your plate with all these kids."

"Pop, I want to get the check today," Dad said.

Granddad chuckled. "Oh no, this is my treat."

Dad got a little tense. "Look, I'm old enough now for you to give me a turn at things. Now, let me get this today. All right?"

Granddad grinned at Dad, closing one eye and tilting his head to the side. "Well, OK, if that's how you want it." They shook on it.

"Good, let's eat," Dad said. He called the boys in from the crab apple tree.

Granddad whistled and lagged behind. He pulled Patrick aside and slipped him a hundred dollar bill.

"What's this?" Patrick said.

"*Top secret,*" he whispered. "Don't tell your Dad. But give this to your Mom tomorrow when your Dad's at work and tell her it's for the meal today. OK?"

"OK, but what about my present?"

"Oh … that … well, I'll tell you about that later."

✦✦✦✦

Inside the lobby the salt-and-peppery aroma of fried chicken mingled with cigarette smoke and laughter. Hungry customers waited in leather sofas and chairs sipping cocktails, listening for someone to call their name. Children crowded around the birdcage containing the two lovebirds from which the restaurant took its name. They were old lovebirds that no longer nipped at the fingers wiggled in their cage. Patrick pressed his nose against the cage and read the plastic plaque:

"THE TWO LOVEBIRDS."

"WHO DO YOU LOVE?"

He wondered what Ebby was doing. He imagined that her family would already be eating in the dining room and he would be assigned a seat next to her. Then he would ask her to pass the honey butter.

"Patrick, don't get bitten," Dad said.

Granddad slipped the maître d' with slicked-back hair a ten dollar bill and suddenly the man spoke out, "Cantwell party, your table is ready … Cantwell…."

The family walked down the chandeliered hallway of the old mansion, past side rooms with glimpses of other families already eating. On the right side of the hallway, the kitchen door swung open. A waiter shot out in a whoosh of steam. He was shouldering a tray heaped with fried chicken. They fell in behind him inhaling the greasy goodness as they went. Mom straightened the boys' hair on the run before they entered the main dining room.

More than a hundred people in their Easter best sat eating and talking, girls giggling, silverware clanking, ice cubes jangling in crystal glasses. There were gunshots of laughter left and right from knee-slapping, old men. Everything was beach bright from the white tablecloths and the sunlight flooding in three walls of French windows. The best tables were by the open windows overlooking the valley and train tracks below. Sister Jenny brought up the rear. She kept her eyes forward, but was unable to ignore the enormous activity and color and reckless happiness of the outside world.

The maître d' signaled two waiters who rapidly cleared some tables, pushed them together, and unfurled fresh tablecloths along a stretch of open window. Granddad pulled out a chair for Nana, and then stood at the head of the table and waited until everyone was in their place and seated. Then he nodded thanks to the maître d' and looked around to see if any old business associates whose names he needed to remember were present.

"Sit down, Joe," Nana said, "Everyone's noticing you."

"I helped get this place started, you know."

"We know. Now sit down."

He sat down and the silverware arrived, followed quickly by ice waters and tangy, cold salads. Patrick looked around the room for Ebby, but she wasn't there. The closest person to him was an old man at an adjacent table with psoriasis on his ear lobe.

"Let's eat," Granddad said.

The boys jabbed forks in their salads and started to eat. Granddad scooped lettuce and radish slices in his mouth with absolute concentration, breathing intensely through his nostrils. Nana cut her lettuce before she ate, wondering how to see the owner's wife who sewed dresses. Dad chewed as he counted heads to estimate what it would cost to pick up the check. Mom picked up her fork and said a secret prayer of thanks for the wonderful day and the new baby coming. Sister Jenny took a Saltine cracker from the basket and tore off the wrapper. Feeling weak and off center, she bit into the cracker and stared out the window at the train tracks below.

"Ladies and gentlemen, thank you for coming to the Two Lovebirds ... and Happy Easter ...." Everyone clapped. It was a man in a tuxedo—Quinton "Cash" Bodash who, along with his wife Rose, owned and operated the restaurant. "I want to thank all of you for coming, and to announce that, as a special treat today, my wife has arranged for a spring fashion show and live quartet." He clapped for the four tuxedoed musicians who entered the room, sat down in a corner, and began to play romantic waltzes. The customers applauded, and the sound of women's voices filled the room as they lectured their husbands about their dying wardrobes.

"We should order a dress today," Nana told Granddad.

But before he could answer, a team of servers arrived with the Two Lovebird's famous fifteen-course fried chicken meal. Antique china bowls brimming with mashed potatoes, Spanish rice, peas, carrots, string beans with bacon bits, coleslaw, cinnamon applesauce, fried chicken and more. The bowls were passed around the table and everyone served themselves big spoonfuls of food. Plates overflowed. Forks and knives went to work. The family was quiet and happy. It seemed like the moment Mom was waiting for.

"Excuse me, everyone," Mom said to the table, "May I have your attention? We'd like to make a toast." She smiled at Dad.

Just then, the owner of the restaurant rushed up with a complimentary bottle of champagne for his old friend Granddad Cantwell. "Thanks for the tip on that stock," Bodash whispered.

A cork was popped and champagne poured for the adults, all wondering what was about to be said. Sister Jenny was watching Teddy move his mashed potatoes with a spoon to hide his string beans from view. She guessed that the toast was about another pregnancy. She ate her Spanish rice and remembered her lost love and the family they might have made together. Tears stung her eyelids, and she put down her fork.

"I'd like to propose a toast," Dad said, "to all of us, our family, and … *the new baby* on the way."

Granddad leaped to his feet, lifted his glass and raised his voice to be heard in the entire banquet room. "Hey, everybody, a toast to my fourth grandchild who I just learned is on the way. And to my son, a great man."

The crowd all clapped and raised their glasses. Husbands laughed. Wives turned to get a better view of Mom's stomach. Children across the room raised the milk glasses imitating their parents. The band played "Rock a Bye Baby." Mom started to cry. Dad beckoned her up and started to dance with her. Sister Jenny grabbed a glass of champagne and guzzled it, then asked the waiter for more. She took another gulp, picked her fork back up and began stuffing herself with fried chicken, mashed potatoes, and a roll dripping with honey butter. Her long fast was over. Then the champagne flamed in her stomach. She paused to look out at the train tracks. Just a few short steps and she could dive out the window. She stood up. Her head felt dizzy and her mouth flushed with saliva. She held a napkin to her face and contained the first short burst. With the band playing merrily, Mom and Dad dancing and hugging and everyone clapping and toasting, Patrick was the only one who noticed the barf chunks on her chin.

- chapter fourteen -

"WHERE DID SISTER JENNY GO?" Mom said.

"I don't know," Dad said, looking around.

"Pass the mashed potatoes," Granddad said.

"I have to go to the bathroom," Patrick said.

"All right, but hurry back," Mom said.

"Don't miss the fashion show," Nana said.

Inside the ladies room, the owner of the restaurant, Rose Bodash, discovered the thin nun crying by the basin. The vomit had splashed down the front of her white habit. Without asking questions, Mrs. Bodash helped Sister Jenny clean up and led her to the servant's elevator. They rode upstairs to an unused room with a bed, a dresser and a chair.

"Give me your clothes, and we'll run them through the quick cycle," Mrs. Bodash said.

Dazed and quiet, Sister Jenny undressed down to her underwear. She folded her arms across her chest and stood in the middle of the room as the harsh sunlight scorched through a window covered with sheer white drapes. "There should be a robe in the closet, dear," Mrs. Bodash said. She bundled up the soiled clothes and got back on the elevator. The elevator door closed, and Sister Jenny was alone. She turned and saw herself in the full-length mirror. The girl who used to smile back at her was gone and in her place was a skinny, miserable looking thing covered in goose bumps.

Downstairs, Patrick wandered around looking for Sister Jenny. He felt sorry for her. He had never seen a religious person throw up before. He looked in the kitchen where two black cooks were laughing and sizzling chicken breasts in big pans. He looked in the waiting room where more families were drinking cocktails and listening for their names. He went down a side hallway and opened a door where he saw Mrs. Bodash cranking the knob on a washing machine. He went farther and opened another door. A group of beautiful women in bras and underwear was putting on clothes for the fashion show. One lady was trying to pull a zipper up her bare back. She looked over her shoulder with a cigarette bobbing in her mouth.

"Hey kid, will you dance with me today?" she said. The women all laughed and he closed the door.

Upstairs in the bedroom, Sister Jenny heard voices coming down the hallway. She hid in the closet and waited, crouched like an umpire and watching through the keyhole. A man and woman wheeled in a rack of dresses swinging on hangers. The man closed the door. It was quiet. Sister Jenny watched them. The man kissed the woman. They fell on the bed and kissed some more. The woman was laughing like when a dog is licking you and you want it to stop, and the man told her to stop laughing, because he was *crazy* about her, and he was *only in the stupid fashion show to be near her.*

"You're *near enough,*" she said.

The man kept up his campaign, but suddenly, the elevator in the hallway dinged. The couple leaped off the bed and left the room. The elevator door opened. It was Mrs. Bodash. She looked in the room, but didn't see Sister Jenny who was frozen in the closet.

Patrick gave up trying to find Sister Jenny. He walked back across the dining room past the row of women modeling dresses to the sound of the string quartet. The music made him think about Ebby. It was ideal music for the new thing.

"Did you see Sister Jenny?" Mom said.

"No, she must be in the bathroom. I think she got sick."

"*Sick?* Really?" Mom tossed her napkin on the table and got up to go look for her.

"It must be the fast," Dad said.

"It's torture what they do to these young nuns," Granddad said, pulling out a cigar.

Nana glared at him. "Joe, don't smoke that now ... *the fashion show!*"

"Honey," he laughed and waggled his cigar at her, "this is the only way I can get through the fashion show."

Granddad got up from his chair and sat on the ledge of the open window overlooking the valley and the train tracks. He lit up, as the master of ceremonies called out the categories of dresses.

"And now, for the younger set, it's the Beatles' look."

The band played "I Want to Hold Your Hand." John put down his fork and shook his head. "That's really cruddy. That's not the way it goes. That's cruddy."

Taking advantage of the commotion, Teddy grabbed a handful of string beans and dropped them under the table on the rug.

"Patrick, come here," Granddad said, "I want to show you something."

Patrick looked at Dad for permission, and he nodded. Patrick got up and stood by the window ledge where Granddad sat.

"Look," Granddad said.

"What?" Patrick said.

"I wanted you to share my view." Below were the railroad tracks that ran along the Meramec River. The hills were light green and white with spring. Granddad's cigar smoke played in the free air.

"I thought you were gonna give me my present," Patrick said.

Granddad squirmed. "Oh, that … Well, I had a plane for you, a really good wind-up airplane, but it got stuck in a tree back at the nun's place."

"Oh."

"Don't worry. We'll get it later after the wind frees it. Here, let me give you something for today." Granddad took off his wristwatch and put it on Patrick's wrist. It was too big. Patrick held it to his ear. "It's a good watch. Keeps good time. It's not expensive. But I've had a lot of times with that watch. A lot of years."

"Thanks, Granddad."

"You're welcome. You can stick it in a drawer until you get older and it fits. Maybe someday you'll be working downtown and you can look at that watch and think it used to tick on my arm."

Patrick nodded and held it to his ear.

Granddad studied the train tracks below as a freight train struggled through the valley, as far away as a toy. The caboose was getting near. He discreetly shot a quick spit out the window. "It's a marvelous thing, your mother having another baby."

"Yeah," Patrick said leaning forward to spit. His effort fell short and landed on the ledge. Granddad pretended not to notice.

"It's a beautiful view, but I don't know where the time went," Granddad said.

The crowd applauded gently as the garden party dresses strolled in. Yellow-and blue-dressed girls paired off with college-aged male models for a walk around the string quartet. Granddad puffed slowly, hoping his cigar would last. Then something happened that made everyone stop eating. One of the spring dress models drifted out of line and began to waltz with her man. She pulled and swung him in wide circles that narrowly missed a busboy. Her dancing was honey-butter smooth, and she filled the room with excitement. Younger women smiled dreamily and reached for their husband's hands while aging men leaned over and squeezed their wives' flabby arms.

"We ought to buy you *that* dress," the man with psoriasis on his ear said to his wife.

Mom came back and sat down at the table. She turned to look at the fashion show. She shot a funny look at Dad, who was doing some math on a napkin. She looked again at the model stealing the show. Then she found her purse and put on her glasses.

"It's her," Mom said.

"It's who?" Dad asked.

"Her." Mom pointed.

It was Sister Jenny, out of uniform, dancing. She had slipped on the dress intended for the other woman upstairs. Then, wandering around the hall in a weakened state, she was bumped and jostled into the undertow of the fashion show, where her feet automatically returned to the steps she once danced with the love she'd left behind.

summer

- chapter fifteen -

IN THE SUMMER TIME the train tracks became a wild place—hot, noisy with bugs, hemmed with prairie grass, lady cigar trees and scrub brush. The tracks were ugly, and the tracks were beautiful. A butterfly might whirl out of the scrub brush over the rails. A blue jay might squawk in and eat it. Useless things littered the tracks—dead Christmas trees still glistening with tinsel, junk tires, unredeemable soda bottles. Sometimes a hobo would appear. He would rise out of the earth on the horizon like an apparition, an anonymous man, shimmering in the heat waves between the rails. Parish golfers on the bluegrass fairway next to the tracks would notice the hobo. Holding a wet Pepsi bottle to his neck, a golfer might stare and wonder. *Where did he come from? Where did his parents go wrong?* The golfers would swat their balls and hurry down the fairway. It was against the law to be a hobo. A sign by the bridge clearly warned:

OFF LIMITS. NO TRESPASSING.
PATROLLED BY RAILROAD POLICE.

But one sign could not silence the inviting sound of trains on the tracks. It was music that could be heard for miles. The engine horns, the struggling moan of the diesels combusting, the rackety rhythm of the boxcars rocking—it reached the ears of parish boys bored with summer and they sped toward the tracks like ants to spilled ice cream. They climbed the embankments and parted the scrub brush to see the trains. When the last boxcars and caboose hurtled by, the after-breeze cooled them. The tracks were comfortable. There were no rules up there. It was a sermon-free, catechism-free zone. It was a world of this summer, this day, this stolen cigarette, this passing train—it was *the tracks.*

Patrick emerged from the scrub brush at the top of the embankment by the train bridge. He stood at the exact spot where he had jumped in front of the train with Ebby. But he wasn't thinking about that. He hadn't seen her all summer. He was looking behind him laughing. His brother John and a friend were running up behind him, still hidden in the tall brush. Patrick turned his head toward the tracks and froze.

A hobo was right in front of him.

He was a whiskered man in dirty clothes. The wooden handle of a pistol peeked above his belt line. In one hand he held a red-and-white striped pouch of Beechnut chewing tobacco, and with the other, he was shoveling it in his mouth like brown manna. His right cheek bulged, and his teeth were dog mean and dingy. Patrick stood still staring at him.

"What the hell are *you* looking at?" the man said.

Patrick whipped his head aside and stared at a tangle of weeds at his feet. The hobo kept walking. Patrick sneaked a glance back at him and saw he was crossing the bridge. John and his friend thrashed out of the scrub brush.

"Guys!" Patrick whispered sharply. He pointed at the man. They all looked at him. He was spitting to the side and heading down the straightaway toward the horizon where the heat made the tracks wiggle.

"Who's that?" John whispered.

"I don't know," Patrick said, "Maybe we should get off the tracks. Dad told me—"

John's friend interrupted. "Oh, that's just some bum. He won't hurt nobody. I seen them before. They steal stuff out of the boxcars when they stop. Besides, if your Mom hadn't kicked me out, we wouldn't be here."

He was right. Mom had kicked him out. His name was Kurt Logan, and he was John's older friend. He was a tough kid with burly cheeks and the longest hair in grade school. Kurt was a fourth-grader who was already eleven, because he had to repeat a couple grades. His parents were divorced and always moving. Children looked to him as an example. He got in trouble at school and knew cuss words that mattered. His latest word was "turd." Dad said Kurt Logan was "a bad seed." He was always getting younger boys to do bad things. Like last night. Kurt had spent the night because his mom was working and she was afraid he might burn down her house if she left him home alone. He had come up with the idea to put a rubber band around the trigger of the sink-mounted dish sprayer. When Dad turned on the faucet to rinse his cake plate, the sprayer blasted him in the stomach.

"*What the hell?*" Dad said. The boys laughed. Dad told the boys and Kurt to get right to bed. "That Kurt Logan is a Peck's Bad Boy," Dad said to Mom.

"Well, honey, he's from *a broken home,*" Mom whispered, "Maybe our boys will be a good influence on him." After the lights went out, Patrick got in bed with his Wolfman model, while John and Kurt sneaked out the bedroom window onto the porch roof. Dad had told Patrick and John to *never ever* go out on the roof because they might fall and get killed. But Kurt said it was OK because parents don't know everything. Kurt and John sat out there puffing a cherry Swisher Sweet cigar that Kurt had brought and talking about starting a band. Mom was below feeling the new baby kick while she watched *Peyton Place,* and Dad read a book on the Civil War and glanced up at his framed *Battle of the Wilderness.* In the morning Mom came in the room and found a startling scene. Two action figures—Johnny West and his Indian companion—were hanging by their necks from bathrobe belts tied to the bed.

"Kurt Logan, you're *destructive!*" Mom said. "I want you to go home after breakfast."

So, they were on the tracks walking Kurt home. John turned to Kurt with urgent business on his mind. "Before we go, just show it to me now. I'll tell you if it's any good," John said.

"Not now, it's in the *you know what,*" Kurt said.

"Look, you told me last night you could be our drummer. I want to get the band going *this* summer," John said. "Show me the picture, and I'll tell you if it's any good."

"What about the turd?" Kurt said, looking at Patrick.

John looked at his younger brother Patrick. "He's all right. He won't tell anybody."

"Well, he has to do the password first," Kurt said.

"The password?" Patrick said.

John turned to Patrick. "You have to do the password to see the fort. He's got a fort up here with a picture of a drum set we need."

"Make him *do* the password," Kurt said.

"What's the password?" Patrick said.

"You have to stand by the edge of the bridge and pull down your pants," John said.

Patrick looked at Kurt, then back at his brother. "But that's nudity."

"Yeah," John said.

"The cars will see me."

"Just turn your bottom to traffic. No one will recognize you."

"Are you going to do it?"

Kurt laughed at both of them.

"I already did it once. It's just for the first time. It'll help with the band," John said.

John waited to the side with Kurt. Patrick walked to the edge of the bridge and looked down at the street. In the middle of the street was a grassy median filled with thousands of yellow dandelions. A kid with a cloth bag was picking the dandelions. It was Jimmy Purvis. A Country Squire station wagon with a pregnant parish mom rounded the bend on a milk run.

"Hurry up," John said.

"And stand on the ledge. You can't hide behind it," Kurt said.

Patrick stood on the concrete ledge where the bridge met the embankment. It was high up. He looked down at the street and Jimmy Purvis. Jimmy was plucking dandelions and not looking up. Patrick turned his bottom to traffic and looked over his shoulder. He reached for his belt buckle and started to undo it. A car whipped around the bend toward the bridge. It was a 1948 Buick with Herb and Octavia Metzenhoffer. They didn't look up. Patrick unzipped his blue jeans and pulled them down. The air circulated between his legs. He stuck his thumbs underneath the elastic waistband of his underwear to pull it down. A woman's heavy shoes marched under the bridge. Patrick looked down. It was a lady in a battleship grey dress suit walking under the bridge carrying a book. She waved to Jimmy Purvis and said hello. Her voice sounded familiar.

"Hello, Jimmy."

"Sister?"

It was their first-grade teacher who had given the slide show on creation, Sister Lucy. "Yes, it's me, Jimmy. What are you doing?"

"Sister, I didn't know it was you without your clothes."

"Without my clothes? Oh, it's just our new habit. We voted on it. No more black habits. Tell me, what are you doing out there in the middle of the street? Does your mother know what you're doing?"

Patrick stood above them with his pants down, but his underwear in place.

"She knows. My Mom told me to pick a bunch of these. She's making the dandelion wine again. Boy, you sure look different."

"Have you been reading this summer?"

Jimmy picked another dandelion nervously. He hadn't touched a book since May. "Yes, Sister."

A Bi-State bus approached. "I'm proud of you. What have you been reading?" She flagged down the bus.

Jimmy remembered the name of a book his dad had told him to read. "I'm reading *Treasure Island*," he said, "It's all about bank robbers. Don't miss your bus."

The bus hissed to a stop for her. "Bank robbers, huh? Well, see you in the fall. I've got to pay off a late library book. You can't steal anything in this life and get away with it." She got on the bus. Up on the tracks, Kurt and John were getting impatient.

"All the way, turd," Kurt said.

"Hurry up," John whispered.

Patrick pulled down his underwear to his ankles and exposed his buttocks. He watched over his shoulder as the bus with Sister Lucy went around the bend. The bus fumes rose up in the July heat. He looked at the sky and the trees and the ground. Then he looked at the tracks and remembered jumping in front of the train with Ebby. He felt naked and ashamed and started to pull up his underwear.

Jimmy Purvis looked up and saw Patrick. Jimmy put his thumb and finger in his mouth and whistled. He could whistle louder than any kid in grade school. "Hey, Patrick," he yelled, "what are you doing up there, taking a shit?"

Patrick jumped away from the concrete ledge. He whipped up his pants. He stuck his head over the ledge and looked down at Jimmy. "I'm not doing anything. What are you doing?"

"Picking weeds. Mom's giving me fifty-cents a sack. Hey, really, what are you doing up there?"

Patrick looked over his shoulder at John and Kurt.

"Get rid of him," Kurt hissed, *"the fort!"*

Patrick looked back at Jimmy and yelled to him. "I had a bug in my pants. I have to change."

Jimmy yelled up. "Hey, I've got something." He pulled out a little red box and flashed it. "Winstons."

The Winston's changed everything. Kurt Logan hurried over to the concrete ledge and yelled down to Jimmy. "Hey, turd, you want to see our fort?"

✦✦✦✦

The fort was on the other side of the twin tracks inside the scrub brush that grew on the embankment. The air was cooler under the ten-foot tall jungle. And it was darker. The light was green and swirly like the inside of a shambled cathedral. Dragonflies swooped among the top branches. The boys followed Kurt to a foxhole, half-covered with plywood. It was an inviting hole with a dugout shelf cluttered with comic books, spent Twinkie wrappers, a cigarette lighter, a comb and mirror, a little radio and a wild turtle in a box. The boys slid into the hole. Jimmy picked up the turtle. On the bottom of the turtle it said in red paint: "Property of Kurt Logan 1966." Kurt took the lighter and lit some candles. His face glowed greenish yellow.

"Be nice to my turtle. Don't drop him if he pees on you." They all laughed. Jimmy handed it to Patrick. Patrick held it at arm's length and turned it upside down. "Hey, how come you wrote on him?" Patrick said.

"That's so if he gets away, some turd won't try to steal him."

"Where'd you get those candles?" Patrick said.

Kurt put his hands on his hips and looked to the side like he was trying to make up a lie, but couldn't think of any. So he told the truth. "Church."

"You *stole* them?" Patrick said.

"I didn't *steal* them. Those are prayer candles. They were burning at church, so I took them to burn here. It's the same thing." Kurt straightened up the fort like a pirate with unexpected guests. He put on a hat. It was the hat the engineer lost the day Patrick and Ebby jumped in front of the train.

"Hey, that's my hat," Patrick said.

"*Your* hat?"

"Yeah."

"I found it. How could this be your hat?"

Everyone looked at Patrick to hear his argument. But Kurt was much bigger. "Well, just tell me one thing," Patrick said. "How come Jimmy didn't have to do the password?"

"He brought the Winstons."

Jimmy put down his mom's sack of dandelions and got out the Winstons. The boys were quiet and studied his hands as Jimmy tapped the pack upside down on his palm. He opened the foil, double-clutched it, and several cigarettes shot halfway out the opening. He grabbed one with his lips and pulled it out as quick as a dad. Jimmy's dad smoked, so he knew how to handle himself responsibly. He offered them to everyone. Kurt grabbed three. But John hesitated.

"I don't know. You got any gum?" John asked.

"No, no gum," Jimmy said.

"Then I don't want one," John said.

"Me neither," Patrick added.

"You neither?" Kurt laughed, "Hell, you wouldn't want one if we had a whole pack of gum."

"My Dad said if I ever smoke, he's gonna take me down to the lung cancer ward to show me what it does to you."

"Your Dad ... Shit, everything you say is *My Dad* or *My Mom* says. You ever think for *yourself?"* Kurt lit up with a purgatory candle and handed it to Jimmy. Jimmy inhaled without a cough and blew the smoke successfully through his missing-tooth grin.

"How'd you lose that tooth?" Kurt asked Jimmy.

"A train."

"Really? What happened?"

"Our Lionel. My sister threw the caboose at me."

"Let's see the picture of the drum set," John said.

Kurt grabbed the comic book and read the advertisement on the back cover out loud. His reading was a little choppy:

MAKE CASH!

WIN BIG PRIZES!

WITH EASY SELLING AMERICAN BOY SEEDS!

The full-page ad was topped with the smiling black-and-white photographs of three crew cut boys. Beneath each photograph was their name and testimonies: "I sold all mine in two hours," a boy from Cedar Rapids boasted. Below the winning sales boys were pictures of different toys to earn by selling seeds door to door. The prizes included a three-speed bicycle, complete archery set, baseball gloves, flash camera outfits, skin diving set, fishing outfit, transistor radios, three-stage rocket, girl's travel case and the big prize—a six-piece rock and roll drum set.

"What do you think?" Kurt said to John.

"Hmmm, 'ard to tell, the picture is so small. But a six piece ought to be fab," John said.

Jimmy flicked the ashes off his Winston. "Hey, anyone ever tell you, you sound like the Beatles when you talk? I mean the way you say the words. What are you guys talking about?"

"We're startin' a band, man" John said. "We're gonna have a drum set and guitars. We're gonna write songs."

"Write songs?" Jimmy took another puff.

John's voice shifted to a sincere British whisper, as he transported the fort from Webster Groves to Liverpool. "I want to write songs that make people *feel things* all over the world, songs about love and the feelings you feel. It'll take some time, but we're gonna practice 'ard and play for parties, then around high school, we'll get records going and have *an impact on this generation*. I'm not going to grow up and work downtown."

Jimmy inhaled some more and nodded. His practical mind had already dismissed John's Beatle goals. "Hey, my dad works downtown," Jimmy said. "He went to see that new Arch they got. It's 630 feet tall, and they got a room at the top with windows. Makes you feel like the king of the world up there."

"Wow, did your dad go up in it?" Patrick said.

"No, he wanted to, but they only give him a half hour for lunch. He had to get back to work," Jimmy said.

John and Kurt ignored the younger boys. They were studying the fine print of the ad. John read it out loud:

"EVERYBODY WANTS AMERICAN BOY SEEDS. THEY'RE FRESH AND READY TO PLANT. YOU'LL SELL THEM QUICKLY TO FAMILY, FRIENDS AND NEIGHBORS.

(SOME OF THE LARGE PRIZES REQUIRE MORE SALES OR EXTRA CASH AS EXPLAINED IN THE BIG PRIZE BOOK.)"

"*The big prize book?* What's that?" John said, frustrated.

"I don't care," Kurt said, standing up impatiently. "It sounds like a lot of shit. Going door to door, like selling those Cutlass Supreme raffle tickets."

"Hey, who won that car?" Jimmy said, "I sold five tickets and never heard nothing about it."

"You didn't hear? A nun won it, Sister Mathilda," Kurt said.

"Sister Mathilda? She's about a hundred years old!" Jimmy said.

"She's so old she don't even drive it. She's got a cataract," Kurt said.

"Man, why should she win if she's already got a Cadillac?" Jimmy said.

"*Cataract!* Her eyes. She's so blind that new Cutlass just sits there shined up all day with zero miles on it," Kurt said.

"We need a drum set," John said.

"You're right. You're right," Kurt said. "Maybe we should just steal the money and buy a drum set."

The boys stopped dead quiet and looked at Kurt. Kurt snuffed out his cigarette in the dripping wax of a purgatory candle.

"It's a sin to steal," Patrick said.

Everyone looked at Patrick.

"Who do you think you are, *Jesus Christ?*" Kurt said.

Patrick swallowed. A distant train horn sounded.

"You want to sell seeds door to door?" Kurt asked, "like selling those Cutlass tickets? Having everyone say no thanks, no thanks, no thanks? Getting doors slammed? Maybe sell a few to your family and then a *nun* wins it? *That's* a sin. Or picking up dandelions all day and sweating for how much?"

"Fifty-cents," Jimmy said.

"*That's* a sin," Kurt said, staring at Patrick. "You think you're better than me, because I smoke or I stole the church candles. Don't you? You're still afraid of sin. But sin isn't like before. It's not like in that movie *The Ten Commandments* where a bunch of miracles happened and then all those people made a gold cow. Now *that* was sin. That was sin because they had the miracles. They were dumbshits. But look around. There aren't any miracles in Webster."

The train rolled by, sending a hot breeze through the scrub brush that made the light and shadows mix on their faces. The boys looked at John holding the American Boy seed advertisement with the drum set. Jimmy slid his tongue through the gap where his front tooth had been and looked at the fifty-cent sack of dandelions.

"Well, what could we steal?" Jimmy shouted over the train.

Kurt smiled. "Lots of things."

"We better go," Patrick said to John. "Mom said to hurry home."

"We'll go after the train passes," John yelled.

The train brakes hissed. Sparks shot off the wheels onto the rocks. The engineer, in command of three diesel engines, was pulling on the brakes. Thousands of tons of momentum fought against the brakes and complained to keep moving forward. On the older boxcars the sheet-metal skin shifted over the frames, tugging at rivets, twisting and groaning like lung-cancer men afraid to die. The brakes seized the wheels into the rails. The rails pressed into the wood ties. The roadbed compressed into the embankment. The boys could feel it. The fort trembled around them. Patrick covered his ears. The moaning reached a peak, and then it died. The train stopped. The boys looked at each other.

"Let's go look," Kurt said.

Kurt blew out the candles, kissed his turtle on the back, and put it in the box. They hurried up the embankment into the open. The train waited on the far set of tracks. It was big. It was a strange sight to see dead still. Its vertical lines, usually blurred and rushing, were sharp and waiting. The ladder hand grips waited. The slightly open boxcar doors waited. The wheels waited, hot and ticking. Patrick looked up the line. Boxcars stretched for a half a mile. They were autumn-colored cars—orange, yellow and red.

"Why'd it stop?" Patrick asked.

"Must be another one coming. It's waiting so it can switch tracks. C'mon, you turds," Kurt said.

Kurt, John and Jimmy ran across the empty set of tracks to get closer. Patrick held his ground. He watched Kurt climb into the crack of an open boxcar. "C'mon, there's boxes in here. They could be loaded with oil paintings, or drum sets," Kurt said. John and Jimmy reached up. Kurt grabbed their hands, pulling them into the boxcar. They stood in a streak of sun cutting into the open door. Then they stepped out of view into the darkness. Patrick could hear their muffled talking and their shoes scuffing across the floor of the boxcar. They followed Kurt into the back wall of the car where a stack of boxes waited.

"Open one up," Kurt said.

They broke the seal and tore into a box. Kurt lifted up a heavy paper sack and read the label:

BOY IS IT GOOD CAKE MIX

25 LBS. NET

INSTITUTIONAL SIZE

(KEEP COOL AND VENTILATED)

"Shit," Kurt said. He slammed the bag on the floor of the boxcar. It broke open. White cake mix churned in the shaft of sunlight.

Patrick heard the echo of them laughing and coughing. He watched from the far side of the tracks as white powder poofed out the crack in the door. It was like the lye Mrs. Meyer tossed on the dead opossum. He looked up the tracks. Nothing was happening.

"C'mon, you turds, let's check the other side," Kurt said. The three boys cut across the blade of sun, laughing and spitting cake mix, tripping forward. They found more boxes stacked deep in the dark. Kurt tore into one. "Look, it's worth a fortune!" Kurt ran his fingers through a box of costume jewelry. Jimmy tore into another box. "Shit, it's just hats, ladies hats," Jimmy said.

"Those aren't hats. They're Frisbees!" Kurt said.

Kurt, John and Jimmy grabbed a stack of hats and threw them like Frisbees out the door. Patrick watched the hats twirl and fall in the heat. Some fell on the bridge. Some fell on the street below. John ripped open another box, hoping for a drum set, but finding something strange.

"What is it?" Kurt said.

"I have to show this to my brother," John said.

Patrick looked up the tracks. He saw the blue nose of a Missouri Pacific passenger train appear. It had just rounded the corner half a mile up and was coming fast. It's white headlight blurred in the heat. John stuck his head out the boxcar. "Hey, Patrick—"

"*TRAIN!*" Patrick yelled.

John looked and saw it. "*Train!*" he shouted behind him to Kurt and Jimmy in the boxcar.

Kurt grabbed two boxes. "We've gotta get off. Grab what you can for the fort," Kurt said. Jimmy searched for another twenty-five-pound sack of BOY IS IT GOOD CAKE MIX. Patrick ran across the rails to the open boxcar. Kurt jumped out. "Out of the way, turd." He sloshed costume jewelry on the rocks as he ran. Patrick touched the open mouth of the boxcar. It was hard steel like things on Dad's workbench he wasn't supposed to touch. John pulled Patrick up. He stood in the slice of sunlight. Cake mix filled his nostrils.

"I'm not stealing anything," Patrick said.

"I know, but look at this. You've gotta see this. *This* is cool," John said.

Out of a box marked "Defective," John pulled a hairy glob of something. It was a rubber Wolfman mask.

"Coming through," Jimmy said pushing John and Patrick aside, as he dragged a twenty-five-pound sack of cake mix.

"What do you want with that?" John said.

"I don't know. I've gotta steal something," Jimmy said, jumping out of the boxcar and dropping the bag on the rocks. The passenger train horn blasted.

"Don't get killed," John yelled. John jumped out of the boxcar to help Jimmy lift the cake mix. Patrick stayed in the boxcar. He ran his fingers over the Wolfman mask. He'd always had a high regard for the Wolfman.

The passenger train thrust down the straightaway toward the bridge. Patrick pulled the Wolfman mask over his face. He could hear himself breathing inside the rubber. He pulled the zipper down the back of his neck.

"Shit, forget this," Jimmy said, dropping the cake mix between the rails. Jimmy dove into the scrub brush. John looked back at the boxcar for Patrick.

"C'mon!" John yelled.

The passenger train inhaled track. It took the bridge. Again, the horn blasted. John dove into the fort followed by a trail of gravel.

"Where's Patrick?" Jimmy said.

The streamlined engine bulleted through ladies hats and the sack of cake mix. A roar of sugary powder blew through the fort. Kurt ducked and pointed. The boys saw something through the green thicket around the fort. It was a man in a white shirt climbing up the embankment not twenty feet away. They spied over the top of the foxhole at him. The speeding passenger train made the scrub brush bend wildly, but the man moved efficiently through the foliage, carrying only his badge, a camera, and a holstered .45-caliber pistol. He was a Special Agent with the Railroad Police, and his long investigation of hobo activity had led him to the bridge. Now, he moved faster toward the top.

Half a mile up the line, the pivoting inner rails of the switch track clicked open, allowing the idle freight train to change tracks. The engineer, a lonely man whose wife had left him because he was away too much, set aside his paperback, *The Search for Amelia Earhart,* and moved a lever forward. The engine pulled ahead. Heavy steel couplers yanked out the slack like a firing squad—BANG, BANG, BANG, BANG, BANG. The boxcar lurched forward, and Patrick fell backwards on a heap of cake mix.

The end of the passenger train shot by. The Special Agent stepped out of the scrub brush near the fort and saw the rear door of the passenger train swirling white powder and ladies hats in its wake. His jaw muscles tightened as the cake mix bag was sliced in half. Jewelry glinted on the rocks between the rails. Unclipping his holster, he studied the boxcars pulling away. Then he saw it. Standing in the open door of a box car, looking right at him was a Wolfboy. He blinked, grabbed his camera and snapped a photograph.

"Stop, Railroad Police!" he shouted.

Patrick stepped back from the crack in the door. He could see the man in the white shirt and blue tie sprinting across the bridge toward his boxcar. Patrick tried to pull off the Wolfman mask, but it wouldn't budge. The zipper was defective. The boxcar rolled onto the bridge above the street, and the Special Agent sprinted to catch up. Patrick looked toward the door again, but the man was nowhere to be seen. He must have given up.

Then a hand hooked around the metal of the boxcar door. Patrick watched the thick fingers pull the door open wider. He kicked cake mix at the hand. But it kept pulling. The door was getting wider and wider. The Special Agent made a running leap, belly-flopping half inside the box car. His left hand curled around the door frame for leverage, the other clutched a pistol.

"Railroad Police! Don't anyone move."

The Special Agent wriggled forward, getting his torso securely inside. Patrick crouched down low. The train was jogging faster, its wheels thumping over rail seams. His eyes adjusting to the darkness, the Special Agent could vaguely see the form of the Wolfboy against some boxes.

"Don't move. You're under arrest."

Patrick moved as fast as he could. He grabbed a lever, jerked it hard and opened the door on his side—barely enough to jump out into the light.

- chapter sixteen -

MEMBERSHIP HAD BEEN DWINDLING in the Mary Queen of Our Hearts Rosary Club. Due to deaths in the parish and the rise of television, only a few of the old faithful attended the monthly prayer meetings held the first Friday of each month in homes smelling of Mrs. Paul's Fish Sticks. Today, half a dozen widows sat in lawn chairs in the shade around a backyard Virgin Mary statue. Father Maligan was there with his German shepherd's leash tied to his lawn chair. With their eyes closed, the group fingered rosary beads and raised their voices over the passing freight train.

"Holy Mary Mother of God, pray for us sinners, now and at the hour of...."

From out of the scrub brush, a Wolfboy ran forward. He tripped down a slope of poison ivy, then got up and leaped past the Virgin Mary. He ran through a half circle of lawn chairs. The German shepherd sprang up barking. Widows gasped. "What in heaven's name," one muttered. "My medicine," another trembled. Father Maligan's chair fell over as his dog yanked on the leash. The Wolfboy was silent and destructive. He crashed into a waiting tray of RC Colas and Bugle snacks, then vanished around the side of the house.

"Stop, thief!" yelled the Special Agent as he ran out of the scrub brush through the Rosary Club meeting. The priest's German shepherd lunged toward the Special Agent, dragging the empty lawn chair.

Patrick sprinted across the zoysia-perfect lawns of ranch homes that lined the railroad tracks. He ran through a sprinkler and almost slipped in the mud. He was now to the point where his legs were in control. He knew that his legs would soon be crossing the busy, four-lane street with the dandelion median. A Bi-State bus was zooming up the stretch. His legs made their move.

On board the bus, Sister Lucy was returning from the library with her finger marking a page of *The Seven Story Mountain* by Thomas Merton. A Trappist Monk, Merton had written how he gave up women, music, and gourmet food in search of God. Sister Lucy was discussing this with a 60-year old caddy on his way to the golf course. An older man, the caddy lived at a weekly-rate hotel downtown. Today his tongue was gullied with hangover and he wanted a cigarette.

"We're all on a journey," she told him.

The caddy nodded. The bus driver slammed on the brakes.

Sister Lucy and the caddy jerked forward. They looked out the window as a Wolfboy cut across the dandelions.

"What is it?" Sister Lucy said.

"It's a Wolfboy!" the caddy gulped.

The Special Agent ran around the front, as Father Maligan tugged at his dog. "Heel, you bird, heel…." The Special Agent halted to wait for the Bi-State bus to get out of his way. The bus driver, a big woman with fourteen long years until retirement, shrugged, shifted into second, and kept going.

Patrick ran past a backyard woodpile, then onto a side street. On the sidewalk ahead of him was a girl with a baby stroller. It was Ebby.

Ebby Hamilton was walking her new baby sister. She wore a Coca-Cola T-shirt with red-and-white checkered bell bottoms. The red checkers had the reassuring words: THINGS GO BETTER WITH COKE.

Ebby looked at the Wolfboy running toward her. She opened her mouth and released a whispered word that floated in the air with concern.

"Patrick?"

"Can't talk now. Gotta change," he said running past her. He ran through a hedge and slid down into the sewage creek. The Special Agent ran across the dandelion median. Patrick sloshed over some rocks into a sewer tunnel beneath the street. It was cool inside. He looked through a curb grate up onto the street. He could hear the freight train rolling by and see Ebby's feet and the baby stroller. The Special Agent's militarily polished shoes ran up to Ebby. He looked at her smart eyes to see what she knew about the case. She saw his badge and holstered gun.

"There's been felony stealing on the tracks," he panted pointing to his badge, "Special Agent, Railroad Police. Did you see a boy run by here in a mask?"

Patrick listened over the sound of sewer water trickling through his Keds. He waited to hear Ebby's answer. He waited to hear her say it was Patrick Cantwell, and he's in the creek. Why shouldn't she? He had felt the new thing for her. But what did she feel? What was in her heart? To her, Patrick was probably just another boy from school.

"Well, did you see him?" the Special Agent barked.

"Yes."

"Which way did he go?"

Ebby glanced at the creek, and pointed in the opposite direction. The Special Agent ran up the street. Patrick watched Ebby walk away pushing the stroller. The new thing washed over him. A sudden dispatch of mid-day sewage poured out of a side pipe into the tunnel. He danced in it. He wanted to thank her. Maybe dance with her. Maybe even kiss her. He tried to undo the zipper again on the back of the Wolfman mask. But it was still stuck. He felt the front of the mask. He looked out the curb grate for Ebby, but she was gone. He listened. He heard the end of the train pass by. The mask was his now. He had stolen it. He waded down the creek in the cool water. He wasn't sure how he felt about stealing. Mainly he felt the new thing. Ebby had lied for him, and now she filled his heart. He grunted and hunched over and pushed dead limbs out of his way. There could be rats or rattlers or more dead opossums up ahead. But it didn't matter. He was the Wolfman. And it was good.

- chapter seventeen -

BY AUGUST THE PRAIRIE GRASS along the tracks was dry and brown, the scrub brush had curled up from the heat, and Patrick had hardened his heart against following the rules to get into heaven. Gloomy and humbled, Dad drove downtown in his un-air conditioned Falcon through the punishing humidity. His proposal to purchase the BOY IS IT GOOD CAKE MIX COMPANY now looked foolish. The two bags he'd ordered to test the company's distribution system had never arrived even though they assured him the bags had been loaded onto the freight train for delivery.

Mom spent those itchy, pregnant days in front of a little back-and-forth electric fan by the dining room table. She dipped her grocery store S & H Greenstamps on a sponge floating in a bowl of water and then pasted them in a booklet to redeem for a prize. Now and then she looked over at the prize catalogue open to the deluxe pink diaper changing station with drawers, ointment and powder holders, and easy-to-clean padded top. The catalogue fluttered in the breeze from the fan. It was a long process, saving up enough stamps.

John and Patrick complained they had nothing to do. They wanted Mom to take them swimming at the public pool. But Teddy was always taking a nap, and Mom was too big and embarrassed to squeeze into a swimming suit. "Why not let us swim by ourselves?" John and Patrick pleaded, "We could ride our bikes to the pool."

"No, your Dad says it's too dangerous," Mom always said, "He wants you to have parental supervision. Stay in the neighborhood where it's safe. Use your imagination. Do something constructive."

So, they wandered up to the tracks. They stole tomatoes from the gardens along the tracks and threw them at Bi-State buses. It was a moment of perfect happiness to watch the tomatoes leave their fingertips, arch off the bridge, and goosh against the bus windows splattering red pulp and seeds down the sides. If they were lucky, the bus would stop and some passengers would climb out and chase them. But most of the time, the buses just kept going.

As the day wore on, the heat would tire them out and they'd fall into the habit of smoking Jimmy's stolen Winstons, and throwing rocks at soda bottles they'd lined up on the rail and named after nuns. One after one, the nuns shattered and died. The real nuns and the school year were approaching like an unavoidable funeral. The summer was dying. They could sense it in the way the tar inside the cracks of the railroad ties was bubbling up in the heat, gasping off a sweet, petroleum smell that was woozy and comforting, but also a little sad. By fall the tar would be hard, the smell would be gone, and the boys would be back in their desks, learning. Then one day Kurt stood on the hill above them, knee deep in prairie grass, and delivered a sermon.

"We need to do something good for a change," Kurt said, "We should hop a freight and go into town and steal something."

Everyone looked at him.

Kurt's words were dangerous, revolutionary. But in the oppressive 95-degree malaise, and with Kurt's hair hanging over his eyes, the boys listened. They didn't have anything more interesting to do anyway. Kurt explained how his divorced dad had taken him to see a movie for his birthday. It was about a guy who hopped trains and killed Nazis to keep them from stealing the masterpiece oil paintings from France.

"What are Nazis?" Patrick said.

"Don't you know *anything?*" Kurt said, "You *oughta* know. You were chased by one."

"I was? When?" Patrick stole a glance at John.

"The Nazis are the bad guys—the police, the nuns and the priests, anyone who's in charge. The main thing is never give in. Never let them win. And never hop a train that's going faster than you can run. If you do, it might cut your legs off. What d'you say?"

"I jumped on the back of our station wagon when it was going in the IGA parking lot once," Jimmy said, "But my mom said get off or I'll kill ya."

"Can't we just *walk* into town and steal something?" Patrick said.

"No, turd, you have to do it right. It's like stealing that mask, which I still say you stole *by accident*. When are you going to do something good on purpose?"

Patrick swallowed.

John lowered the comic book with the drum set and looked at Kurt. John had read how John Lennon kept the Beatles together through their early conflicts. "Hey, man, we need to all get along. We've got a lot of performances ahead of us."

Kurt spit to the side. Patrick spit to the other side. They decided to get along for the sake of the band, and hop the next available freight into town. They sat on the rail and smoked and waited. When the Winstons ran out, they climbed on each other's shoulders and pulled down lady cigars off the trees. The green ones had to be laid out to cure in the sun. A row of dead lady cigars baked constantly on the concrete ledge of the bridge. The lady cigars smoked up hot and thick, harsher than a Winston, like something resistance fighters might settle for behind Nazi lines.

"Train!" Patrick yelled.

A big freight was coming. It appeared around the bend in the distance. Its nose wiggled like a mirage. Then it broke through the haze and hurtled down the straightaway. "Too fast!" Kurt yelled. The engine roared past them. The hot breeze made them squint. They threw rocks at the coal cars. The rocks ricocheted off the rushing metal. They hid from the caboose. Dust settled. The caboose shrunk away and they waited some more.

++++

Smoked-out and thirsty, they crawled on their bellies across the edge of the golf course driving range toward the drinking fountain. The sign said NO TRESPASSING. MEMBERS ONLY. Golf balls whizzed overhead. "Nazi snipers, keep your heads down," Kurt ordered.

Patrick stole the first cold gulps of ice water. The extra ran down his neck and cooled his shirt. While the other boys drank, Patrick saw the bluegrass fairway. He forgot about trains and Nazis and stealing and saw himself twirling Ebby on the fairway. It had been weeks since he'd seen her. But he could still picture her, waiting for him in her green, plaid uniform skirt.

He took Ebby's hands and started dancing with her in wide circles. Her fingertips were soft, gentle. Her smile was pure. The other boys looked at him dancing by himself, then looked at each other. A golf ball thumped on the fairway beside him. Patrick stopped. A foursome of golfers was approaching, one of them yelling and shaking his driver at the trespasser. Patrick heard their distant yelling and then he heard something else. A freight train was coming.

The boys all heard it.

Jimmy put his fingers in his mouth and whistled full blast. Patrick bowed goodbye to Ebby, and threw the golf ball into the rough. They ran into the scrub brush and waited. The engines rumbled by. As soon as the pistons softened out of range, the boys climbed up to the top of the tracks. They ran up alongside the freight. Big steel boxcars flirted like lazy dance partners. Each boy chased a boxcar. There was laughter and cussing. Loose rocks clattered under foot. Patrick thought about hobos and how Dad would probably be against hopping freights. He would probably say it was too dangerous or against the Ten Commandments. But some things Dads in heavy wingtips just couldn't judge right. Grade school fingers grabbed the paint-chipped rungs. Keds left the earth. The train jerked their arms and swept them along.

Patrick's feet landed on the greasy footrest. He looked around. Nazi sharp shooters could be lurking nearby. Kurt, Patrick, John and Jimmy were escaping together. The train understood. It embraced them and rocked them in the humid, bathwater breeze. They hung on the outside of four separate boxcars and grinned crazily at each other. The bridge and the fort and the golfers and the boredom of the hot summer day slipped away behind them as they rolled toward downtown Webster—afraid, excited, yelling SHIT to each other with lady cigar breath, holding in nervous pee, going places at seven miles an hour.

- chapter eighteen -

THEY JUMPED OFF behind the insurance building, a colonial brick structure where adults calculated risk and typed out accident reports.

"Safe!" Jimmy said, as his feet hit the rocks.

"See, I told you, it's not dangerous," Kurt said, standing between the other set of rails with his back turned to any surprise train that might round the corner unheard and smack him dead. The four boys caught their breath and waited for the freight to pass. The shiny box car wheels, as sharp as cutlery knives, rolled forward ready to slice off an arm or leg in the next town.

"That's our target." Kurt pointed. Alongside the insurance building was Straub's Supermarket, an upscale grocery store with mostly retired shoppers. It was ideal for robbing. "Steal something worth a lot," he said.

The gang pushed open the slow electric door and romped into Straub's where the bald head of Harvey the manager periscoped over the top of the manager's guard booth. They ran up and down the canned goods aisle, looking for something worth a lot. String beans were on sale.

Nana and Granddad were in the coffee cake section. Nana bent over to test the gooey butter cakes by pressing her fingertip into the clear plastic wrap. She had told Granddad to keep a lookout. But he started grabbing her shoulders and trying to kiss her on the neck.

"Joe, not here, we're in the gooey butter section," she said.

The gang ran up to them.

"Hi, Nana! Hi Granddad!" Patrick and John said.

"Boys!" They smiled like they had laid their eyes on the best gooey butter cake ever—grandchildren. "Great to see you," Granddad said. "Is your mother here?"

"No, we came by ourselves," Patrick said.

"You walked all this way?" Nana said.

"Yeah," Patrick said.

"We should give you a ride home. It's so hot out," Nana said.

"We don't need your help. We just got here," Kurt said flipping his long bangs for emphasis.

Granddad pulled out his alligator wallet. "Well, here's a dollar, why don't you all go down to Velvet Freeze and have one on us." He gave it to John and messed up his lengthening hair.

"Thanks," they said.

"Be good," Nana said. Patrick looked at Nana. She smiled as if they might have been friends, had they not been relatives. Then she pulled him aside. "Patrick, tuck in your shirt."

He tucked it in.

She sized him up. "Patrick, are you staying out of trouble?"

"Yeah."

"I've been thinking. You've got too much free time. You need some society lessons. One of the ladies in my garden club has a granddaughter who is signed up for the Monday Club. Do you know a girl named Ebby Hamilton?"

Patrick swallowed. "No."

"Well, I know you can't *stand* girls, but I'd like to arrange for you to go to the Monday Club. You need to start combing your hair and learn how to waltz and hold a fork and get with the New Joe if you want to stay out of prison."

"What's the New Joe?"

She whispered to him sternly. "It's not that Peck's Bad Boy you're with, the one with the long hair. Don't be like him. He's trouble."

Patrick felt like dancing right there in the gooey butter aisle. "I guess you're right," he said, giving in.

"Fine, I'll arrange it today, after my nap. Now, be good." Before he could get away, she leaned over, squeezed his chin, and kissed him right on the lips. Her lips were old. He walked around the Pepperidge Farm bread rack, pulled out his shirt tail, and wiped off his lips. Then he followed the others as they ran past the big-haired cashier lady and out onto Main Street. Now Patrick had a secret—he would soon be dining and dancing with Ebby. He squinted into the sun and smiled.

++++

Main Street was hot and quiet. No one knew a gang of criminals had arrived. The boys walked down the sidewalk. The Ben Franklin man with the sad eyes sat behind the counter ringing up another candy bar. A Yellow Cab was parked under a shade tree, the driver smoking and circling the names of horses on the sports page with a pen. Tommy's Shell station had a car in the bay up on the rack. Wrenches clanged and Tommy yelled cuss words. The barbers sat reading the sports page with a big fan blowing on them. The sporting goods man said *May I help you?* to another customer who was just looking as if the shopper had better get out some money and buy something. Firemen leaned back in wooden chairs with sweaty, cold Pepsi bottles while the radio announced the Cardinals were losing. The shoe repairman who looked like Groucho Marx was working in his window and chewing an unlit cigar. The banker with the silver toupee counted twenties. The Rexall druggist counted allergy pills. Paint peeled on the empty Webster Groves train depot where passenger trains no longer stopped to take businessmen downtown because the men all drove cars or took the bus.

The Velvet Freeze was air conditioned and smelled like sugar cones and hot dogs. "That'll be eighty-four cents," the Velvet Freeze lady said to the boys, scooping vanilla ice cream as she watched the Charlotte Peters show on the black and white TV by the malt mixers. Charlotte Peters was a TV star who lived in Webster Groves and drove a purple Cadillac with power windows. She was dark-haired, vivacious, and could sing. Her husky voice filled Velvet Freeze with a song about a woman telling her man to get out of the house and make her some money.

John paid the Velvet Freeze lady for the four cones and the gang sat down on the blue and pink plastic scoop chairs. They licked their cones and the Velvet Freeze lady kept an eye on them. She was a short, bony woman with a Lilly Munster gray streak, but she was the law. There was a sign by the drinking fountain that gave her authority.

VELVET FREEZE TEEN TIME LIMIT
15 MINUTES

John looked at the word "teen" and couldn't wait until it described him. Being a teenager would guarantee the success of his band—cool instruments, hit songs, and girls, girls, girls.

"Well, how are we going to get that drum set?" John said.

Jimmy sneered. "Oh, will you *get off that drum set?* Nobody from Webster hits it big." He bit into his cone with his lone front tooth. "My dad said the thing to do is work for a living, be a chemical salesman. It sounds boring, but it pays good."

John snapped back at him. "You can be a chump if you want to, but I know what I want."

The gang was quiet after the skirmish. Tommy the mechanic from Shell walked in. Everyone looked at him. He was a stocky man in his late fifties. His face was pink with high blood pressure and his fingers were black in the grooves from working on cars. He inhaled a cigarette and studied the wall menu. It was the same as yesterday and the day before.

"Hey, Tommy," the Velvet Freeze lady said.

"Hot out today."

"What can I get you?"

"Oh … Let me have … one of them hot dogs … with some chili on it … and a Coke."

"Large?"

"Yeah, lots of ice." He got out his money.

The Velvet Freeze lady opened the glass door on the hot dog case. Long suffering, orange wieners simmered and blistered on a slowly turning Ferris wheel of death. She rescued one, laid it on a bun, and splashed on a ladle of chili.

Kurt turned to John. "Hey, John, maybe we don't need to steal. Maybe your Dad will *buy us* the drum set. I mean you see him enough."

"What do you mean?" John said.

"I *mean*, your parents aren't divorced yet. He comes home at night. Does he side with you?"

"*Side* with me?"

"You know, does he smack your mom when she hits you or throws pots at you?"

"Mom doesn't do that stuff!"

"Hell, I'm tryna find out is he *for* you?"

John thought about it. "Dad told me once if I'm ever really in trouble, I can always come to him."

Kurt shook his head and dragged his tongue around his cone. "No, I don't mean that Father's Day crap." He raised his voice. "*I mean will he get you the damned drum set?*"

The Velvet Freeze lady and Tommy the mechanic looked over, and blinked, then looked at each other. The boys looked at John. John seemed in doubt. He slouched in the plastic scoop chair. Then he whispered, "No."

"Why not?" Kurt said.

John watched his cone. A dribble of vanilla hit the table. "He told me the Beatles are just a phase. Like pretending I was Superman or Tarzan. He said guitar playing is just a hobby, and that I should read a good book. He told me to read *Treasure Island*."

Jimmy leaped from his chair. "That's the same book my dad told me to read!"

"Sit down, Jimmy," Kurt said.

Tommy paid the Velvet Freeze lady a dollar-twenty-four and grabbed the brown paper sack. He pushed open the door and stepped out into the heat. On the sidewalk he looked in the window at the boys, as if to remember his own summers. But glancing back was not the same as being young. He turned and started walking toward his garage. He had to get that transmission back in by five o'clock.

The boys looked at John. John was quiet. Not licking his cone, John stared at the sign marked "Teen Time Limit." Patrick knew how John felt about the band.

"I wish we could just rob the bank and buy the drum set," Patrick said.

The boys looked at Patrick. Kurt laughed and swung his bangs over his eyes. "You're so full of shit. You're just saying that shit 'cuz you get it from me."

Patrick looked to John for support. "Hey, man, leave my brother alone," John said.

"All right, but I'm sick of him tagging along, wasting Winstons that he only puffs. *You see him dancing today?* He couldn't steal nothing. He couldn't even sneak a candy bar from Ben Franklin."

Patrick's cone broke in his grip. The ice cream ball fell on the floor. "I could so. I could take all the money from Ben Franklin."

"Well, why don't you?" Kurt said.

They looked at Patrick. Patrick looked at the Velvet Freeze lady. But she hadn't heard anything. She was watching the TV and wiping her counter with a wet rag. On the TV, Charlotte Peters swung into her big finish, singing that her man needed to hurry up already and get her that money. Charlotte threw in a lot of hip movement and shimmery dress appeal. The studio audience loved it. They clapped and Charlotte took a bow. One thing Charlotte could always do, was sell a song.

- chapter nineteen -

BUSINESS WAS SLOW at Ben Franklin. The man with the sad eyes sat behind the cash register with his elbows on the candy counter, talking on the phone with his wife about bills. Patrick pushed open the front door. The bell tinkled. The man hung up the phone and looked at Patrick.

Across the street, Jimmy ran up the spiral staircase to his lookout atop the hobby shop parking garage. It was Jimmy's job to whistle in case of trouble. He put a red-hot jawbreaker in his mouth and sucked on it. The red-hot chemicals coated the crevices around his missing tooth. It burned the lining of his mouth. He looked down on Main Street. He could see the bank, the corner Rexall, and the Ben Franklin. A black dog trotted across the street with his tongue hanging out.

John and Kurt ran down the alley between Velvet Freeze and the dry cleaners. They found the back screen door to Ben Franklin unlocked as usual.

"How are you today?" the man asked Patrick.

"Fine."

"School starting soon?"

Patrick nodded and acted like he was studying candy bars. Kurt and John sneaked in the back door. They eased around the corner past the Cut-Your-Own curtains section. They could see Patrick up front by the candy counter and the Ben Franklin man talking to him. Patrick pretended to listen.

"Yeah, back to school," the Ben Franklin man said, "You probably don't want to go." He opened a fresh box of Payday candy bars. And then with a mixture of nostalgia and disgust he said, "Summer, summer, summer ... It can't last forever. Nothing to do … idle time. Besides, these are your formative years. Everything you do is like a building block. That's why school is so important."

"Yeah," Patrick nodded, staring at a row of Milky Ways.

Across the street Jimmy saw the front door of the bank swing open. A man in black wearing an old fashioned straw hat stepped out.

It was Monsignor O'Day.

He was headed for the Ben Franklin. Jimmy spit out his jawbreaker and put his thumb and finger in his mouth to whistle. But his saliva was too red hot and ropey. Spit splattered all over his fingers, but no whistle sound would come.

John and Kurt crawled on their bellies into the tin Jell-O mold aisle. The Ben Franklin man lectured Patrick.

"My nephew goes to that Catholic school, Mary Queen of Our Hearts. We … my wife and I, never had kids. But I spend a lot of time with my nephew. I got him some Lincoln Logs. Now that's a good toy. Lincoln read a lot of books when he was your age. He'll be starting scouts this fall, my nephew. You Catholic?"

Patrick looked up at him.

Kurt pushed over the tin Jell-O mold display. An avalanche of heart-shaped, bird-shaped, angel-shaped Jell-O-ware clattered to the floor.

The Ben Franklin man ran to the back of his store. Patrick leaned over the counter and pressed NO SALE.

Jimmy kept trying to whistle as Monsignor O'Day strode down the sidewalk toward Ben Franklin.

Kurt and John ran out the back door.

Patrick reached into the drawer. He felt something. It was beads in the half-dollar compartment—rosary beads. The phone behind the counter rang. Patrick looked down the aisle. The Ben Franklin man would be coming to get the phone. Patrick picked it up.

"Ben Franklin," Patrick whispered.

The voice on the other end spoke. "This is Ebby Hamilton again on that yellow fabric I need for the Monday Club. My mom said to call and check."

Monsignor O'Day stopped in front of Ben Franklin. He turned around to see who was calling him. It was the banker with the silver toupee leaning out of the front door of the bank. Monsignor had been doing card tricks for all the lady tellers.

"Monsignor, you forgot your cards," the banker yelled. Monsignor patted his shirt pocket where the cards belonged, then shook his head at his forgetfulness.

He turned around and headed for the bank.

Jimmy unzipped his pants to pee on the overhead parking lot wall. The pressure had gotten to him. He watched Monsignor walk back to the bank, and, losing track of his aim, peed on his shoe.

"Your yellow fabric for the Monday Club?" Patrick said.

"Who is this?" Ebby asked. *"Is this Patrick?"* The melody of her voice saying his name made him feel the new thing. He felt ashamed of the robbery and the train hopping and throwing tomatoes at buses.

The Ben Franklin man was stumbling over Jell-O-ware. Patrick had to get off the phone.

"Ebby, I'm sorry, I have to go. We're real busy here." He hung up. He looked at the cash drawer, beyond the rosary beads, to the rows of green currency. He was tempted to give up crime, to go clean. But he remembered Kurt teasing him and how much the drum set and the band meant to John. He grabbed the cash, shut the drawer, and ran out the front door.

- chapter twenty -

THE BOYS HEARD SIRENS AS THEY RAN down the tracks for the
fort. So they ran faster. To stay out of sight they took the low road by the
crossing gate. They cut across the fifth green at the golf course where older
women with nothing defrosted for dinner were taking gimmies and talking
about maybe going out to eat. The boys splashed through the creek that trickled
through a big arching sewer tunnel under the tracks. They cut through some
back yards and heard a siren coming down Main Street right for them. They saw
a little girl playing tea and ducked into her playhouse. She ran out yelling for
her mom. The siren flew past them. It was a fire truck. Teacups fell off the table,
as they scrambled out of the playhouse and climbed the embankment onto the
tracks. In the distance, by the bridge, they could see the smoke. It was a big fire.
The scrub brush was burning.

"*The fort!*" Kurt yelled.

They sprinted across the tracks and ran down the golf course fairway.
Golfers and greens keepers and aproned-housewives were running toward the
fire. The boys blended in with the crowd. Big-fendered, red fire trucks were
pulling up along the straightaway. Firemen shot water into the burning bushes.
The flames soared fifteen-feet high. White smoke curled and rolled in the heat
down the tracks. They ran up to a firefighter.

"What happened?" Jimmy said.

"GET BACK! STAY BACK!"

They stepped back.

"What happened?" Kurt yelled.

"Sparks from the train wheels! This brush is all dried out. *Now, stay back.*"

"C'mon," Kurt yelled.

They ran down a side street to the base of the bridge. The smoke was so thick they could barely see across Main Street. They heard a puttering sound. The front end of a Volkswagen Beetle cut through the smoke. It kept going. Patrick closed his eyes, and they chanced it across the street. The smoke thinned a little. They could see the embankment hiding the fort had already burned up. It was drenched wet and hissing, nothing left but black ashes and stubble sticking through the ground. A fire truck pulled away to chase the flames up the straightaway. They ran up the embankment through the smoke for the fort. It was gone—the plywood roof, the comic books, the purgatory candles all gone. Nothing was left but a foxhole in eye-stinging smoke.

"Damn," Kurt said, and then he screamed, *"My turtle!"*

Kurt picked up a black clump of dead, burnt turtle. He turned it upside down. It was still marked: PROPERTY OF KURT LOGAN 1966. The boys stood by the tracks. Their eyes were watery and they coughed in the smoke. It was like a parish barbecue when Father Maligan burned all the pork steaks. A fireman in a white shirt emerged out of nowhere. He was holding something. They looked at him. It was a box of stolen costume jewelry with the Wolfman mask on top. It had been in the fort. They looked at the man again. It was the Special Agent, Railroad Police. He dropped the box and rested one hand on his holster.

"Don't anybody run this time."

- chapter twenty-one -

PATRICK'S INTERROGATION ROOM at the Webster Groves Police Station had a wood table and an orange vinyl sofa against one wall. Above the sofa was a wire glass window looking into the lobby. Previous prisoners had picked holes in the vinyl sofa. Patrick picked at the holes while the Special Agent stood over the table and opened a briefcase. Patrick was afraid of the Special Agent, but he tried not to show it. The Special Agent crushed out a non-filter cigarette in the ashtray. He breathed pensively through his nose as he laid some photographs on the table. They were glossy black and whites of a Wolfboy riding a boxcar. He looked at Patrick.

"Take off your shoes."

Down the hall in a separate room, Kurt was refusing to speak. The police sergeant threatened him with reform school and a life in the Missouri prison system. He slapped a yardstick on the oak table. But Kurt kept quiet. Kurt wore a grimace with a slight thrill in his eyes as he watched the blue uniform of the Webster police sergeant transform into a Nazi uniform.

"Tell me zee extent of your activiteez," he heard the officer say.

John was in another room with a blonde police officer. She was beautiful. She sat across the table from John fingering her bangs as she wrote on a yellow tablet.

"I guess Paul," she said, "if you really have to know, Paul would be my favorite Beatle. But, please, we need to concentrate on the robbery at Ben Franklin today. "

"Why don't you like John Lennon best?" he said.

And across the hall in the chief's office, Jimmy was reclined in a leather chair. Jimmy had cracked. The chief handed him a tissue to wipe his eyes. Then he offered him an Oh Henry candy bar left over from the police fundraiser.

"Don't worry, kid, just tell me exactly what happened, and you'll all be on probation a year. Stay out of trouble, and you might still be a chemical salesman some day."

"It all happened so fast," Jimmy said, "One day I was picking dandelions...."

Patrick took off his Keds. The Special Agent removed from his briefcase a hunk of plaster—a cast from a mud print left behind by the Wolfboy. He held Patrick's right shoe up to the plaster and studied it. He looked at Patrick.

Out by the front desk a troubled man walked in. It was the man from the Ben Franklin. The lady dispatcher told him the boys were in custody, and if he could have a seat, she would bring them together for identification. He sat down in the waiting area and heaved a sigh. He looked at the clock. It was going on five. He reached for a magazine. It was the August edition of *Boy's Life*. On the front a crew cut boy smiled above the caption: "Today's Cub Scout."

The Special Agent wetted the bottom of Patrick's shoe with an ink roller and made a print on a piece of paper. He blew on the print to dry it. Then he put the print and the plaster cast in his briefcase. The door swung open. It was the lady dispatcher leading the other boys in. She handed the Special Agent some papers.

"Notes from the other boys' interviews, sir."

He nodded to her. The boys sat on the vinyl sofa next to Patrick. The Special Agent looked at them. He read the notes. He breathed deeply and exhaled. The door opened again. It was the dispatcher with the man from Ben Franklin.

"Yes?" the Special Agent said.

"Sir, this man's store was robbed this afternoon by some boys who broke into his cash register."

The Special Agent nodded.

The man from Ben Franklin leaned his head in reluctantly. His sad eyes were red and puffy. He looked different away from the candy counter—older. In his hands was the Boy's Life magazine all twisted up tight. He looked at the boys. He looked at Patrick.

"Oh, boys," he said, as if it were his fault, "Why did you do it?"

"How much is missing?" the Special Agent asked.

"About twenty-two dollars."

"Empty your pockets boys," the Special Agent said.

They emptied their pockets. Jimmy dropped a red sparkly Super Ball. The Special Agent stared forward as it ricocheted off the walls and table, but never hit him. It landed in the metal trashcan and rattled to its death. Kurt put his wallet on the table. The Special Agent opened it. No money. Just two pictures, two separate photos, one of his mom and one of his dad. John had sixteen cents change from Velvet Freeze. Patrick put a clump of dollars on the table.

"Count it," the Special Agent said.

The man from Ben Franklin counted it. He swallowed and looked at the Special Agent. "Twenty-two dollars."

"You can take your money," the Special Agent told the Ben Franklin man, "I'll note it in the report."

The man from Ben Franklin folded the money in half and turned to leave. But he paused and turned to the boys. "Why did you do it, boys? Wasn't I nice to you? I never made any money off the candy. It was just there for you. Just so you'd have some place to go … some place for boys to be boys."

He left. The interrogation room was quiet. Jimmy started to cry again, but Kurt jabbed him in the ribs. The Special Agent put the reports in his briefcase and snapped it shut.

"*Good Catholic boys,*" he said. He shook his head, walked out, and closed the door.

- chapter twenty-two -

THE TWO CITY WORKERS who had once shoveled up the dead opossum ran into the police station. They had been putting rubber sealant on the pavement around the Webster swimming pool—over by the deep end where the high school girls in bikinis laid out—when they heard the news.

"Did some kids really rob the bank?" the fat one said.

"No, they robbed the Ben Franklin," the lady dispatcher said.

The skinny one with the smoker's cough looked at the clock. It was after five. "I hate to work late. Can we get a look at them?"

"Stick around. Their parents are supposed to pick them up," the lady dispatcher said.

Inside the interrogation room the boys knelt on the couch and looked through the wire glass window into the lobby at the dispatcher and the two city workers.

"What will happen to us?" Patrick said.

"You mean what will happen to *you?*" Kurt laughed. "You're the one caught holding the money."

"Shut up," John said shoving Kurt against the sofa.

Kurt got back up. "I could beat the shit out of you all right now," Kurt said, "But there's probably hidden cameras."

Jimmy stood apart—on the other side of the table away from the gang. He'd retrieved his Super Ball from the trash and was bouncing it on the table. "We'll be all right. The chief told me."

"The chief told you what?" Kurt said, *"Did you talk?"*

"He told me we'll be on rotation for a year, and if we stay out of trouble we won't go to reform school."

"*Reform school?*" Patrick said.

The boys watched Jimmy bounce his Super Ball. It bounced again and again like it was counting off the years they could lose behind bars. Then he stopped. Jimmy could see through the wire glass that his mom and dad were in the hall by the dispatcher. He put the Super Ball in his pocket. "Oh, hell, I'm in shit now," he said. The other boys kneeled on the couch and spied at Mr. and Mrs. Purvis. Jimmy's mom, who had been sipping dandelion wine and watching *Days of Our Lives,* was still red-eyed from crying. Jimmy's dad looked explosive. He wore a black suit, having cut short an important abrasive chemical sales call to come to the station. The lady dispatcher walked toward the interrogation room and opened the door.

"James Purvis?"

Jimmy looked at the gang, then tried to work up some crying again. He crossed the threshold into the lobby. The door shut. The gang looked through the wire glass. Jimmy's mom started crying and reached out her arms. Jimmy moved toward her, but his dad stepped forward and cracked him on the back of the head. He shouted for Jimmy to stand up straight and not move an inch while he signed some papers. The city workers lurked nearby dusting the clock with a rag.

"*Man!*" Patrick said.

Jimmy's family left, and Kurt's mom appeared. She was a cross-eyed woman with poodle hair and a cigarette in her mouth.

"Where is he?" she yipped.

Kurt saw it was his turn. "I'm glad it ain't my dad. This'll be a cinch, guys."

The door opened.

"Kurt Logan?"

Kurt winked at the lady dispatcher. He flipped his hair back and glanced at John and Patrick. But before he could step into the hallway his mom stepped into the doorway. She unzipped her purse and pulled out a pair of scissors.

"Turn around," she snapped.

"Mom!"

"*DO IT,*" she yelled. "Damned, crazy kid."

Kurt turned around and took a breath. Mrs. Logan bit her cigarette, grabbed his hair and started cutting. Big chunks fell on the floor. She kept pumping the scissors faster, cutting closer to the scalp to reshape him into the boy who once obeyed. Then his mom got winded from the excitement and started to sob. Her lips quivered and her cigarette fell on the floor. Wiping mascara across her face, she told Kurt to apologize to the police and follow her.

Kurt said he was sorry, but then he threw in a little grin like he had seen the resistance fighters do right before they're lined up in front of a brick wall and executed by Nazi machine gun fire.

"Damned kid. Just like your father. You're cleaning the downstairs toilet, and you ain't never…."

Her voice trailed off as she led him out of the station. The city workers busted up laughing and poked and slapped each other. The big one grabbed the skinny one's hair and pretended he was cutting it with a scissors. "This is better than Wrestling at the Chase," the skinny one said coughing uncontrollably. "Are there any more?"

"Two more," the dispatcher said.

"All we need is chips and beer," the fat one said.

John and Patrick's Dad walked in wearing his grey suit and tie uniform from his executive job at St. Louis Foods. The boys watched through the wire glass. He looked pale, like a church statue. He spoke to the lady dispatcher. He signed the necessary papers with little movement. The skinny city worker started coughing again. Dad looked at him. The worker put his hand with tar stains on Dad's shoulder.

"They're over there," he pointed. "Damned kids these days. It's television. It's not your fault. It's that TV set. And it's that book by that damned Dr. Spock saying you shouldn't hit kids no more. Shit, *my ass you can't.* I mean if you want to knock them around and get it out of your system … What I mean is … it might do them some good." He took his hand off Dad's shoulder and wiped his nose.

Patrick and John watched through the glass as Dad erupted into a thunderstorm of yelling at the city workers. He was red in the face and pointing at them and gesturing like a prosecutor. It appeared the robbery, the fire, and Dad's high property taxes were all the fault of the city workers. They shrunk back and the lady dispatcher motioned for them to go through a door, which they did, and disappeared. Then she came and got the boys.

"John and Patrick Cantwell."

They came out and looked at Dad. He sighed. "C'mon, boys, let's go home."

In the car, Dad, John and Patrick were quiet. They drove down Main Street in front of the Ben Franklin. Dad didn't look over at it, and he didn't say anything. John was in the front seat, Patrick in the back. When they drove past the railroad crossing, the boys could see the gates were down and a slow freight was going through, the last of the day. But they didn't say anything.

"Boys, I don't know what happened. And we're not going to talk about it right away." His voice was soft and hoarse from yelling at the city workers. "Let's go home. I want you two to take a shower and get ready for dinner. Put on clean shirts. Let's have a calm meal. And don't upset your mother with the baby coming." He looked at them to see if they were listening. "You're going to be punished. Don't think this is some small thing. It's a helluva development. John, you're going to have to go to confession. Patrick, what grade are you in?"

"Second."

"You don't go to confession yet, do you?"

"No."

They drove along Main Street beside the railroad embankment. The hills were naked and charred. The scrub brush was burnt clean, except for the roots. A fireman was hosing it down for the night so it wouldn't rekindle. "The main thing I want you both to understand is you're in big trouble, but you're still a part of this family." Dad put on his turn signal.

Tink-tock, tink-tock, tink-tock....

"It's like your Granddad Cantwell said to me when I was a boy. He said, if you're ever really in trouble, you can always come to me, and I'll be there for you because I'm your father. And Nana would say, if I'm ever afraid to go right to my Dad, I can go through her first."

Tink-tonk, tink-tonk, tink-tonk....

"You understand?" Dad said, looking over at John.

John looked at Dad and nodded.

Dad looked in the rear view mirror at Patrick.

Tink-tonk, tink-tonk, tink-tonk....

Patrick was studying the back of Dad's head. His haircut was neatly trimmed above his collar line. He couldn't say it, but he loved his Dad the most at times like this. Whenever he was in trouble, his Dad was always calm, and fair, and attentive. This offered Patrick a strong incentive to stay in trouble, to feel that closeness.

"OK, Patrick? Are you listening?" Dad said.

"OK, Dad," Patrick said.

"Very good," Dad said.

"And Dad," Patrick said.

"Yes, Patrick?"

"You left your blinker on."

+ + + +

Dad pulled in the driveway. They got out of the Falcon and the dog barked at them. They opened the gate and headed around for the back door. Inside, Mom was sitting at the breakfast room table crying. She had her arms wrapped tight around Teddy who wasn't crying. She looked up at Dad.

"It's all right," he said. "Everything's going to be all right. Don't cry. There's going to be a juvenile court hearing, but they'll get a year's probation. I'll just have to work more with them, maybe get them into scouts. Give them something constructive to do with their time. Some direction. They'll be all right."

She kept crying.

"Honey," Dad said. "They'll be fine. They're just boys."

She kept crying and shook her head.

"I just got the call," Mom sniffed and let go of Teddy long enough to wipe her nose. "Granddad called. He said she took a nap, and when he went up to check on her, she was gone."

"Gone?" Dad whispered.

"Nana … Nana is dead."

- chapter twenty-three -

ON THE MORNING OF THE FUNERAL, Grandad parked the Cutlass Supreme in front of a fire hydrant near the Famous Barr store where he had met Nana in the brass revolving doors in 1925. He was alone. Wearing a funeral suit and a vacant grimace, he got out and walked down the rain-soaked sidewalk until he entered the revolving doors and revolved. He revolved back to 1925. A memory of Nana floated in from the summer sidewalk. She was wearing her hair in a bob with a white bow. They bumped into each other in the same compartment of the revolving door. She smiled awkwardly. They both laughed and kept revolving. They realized they had once been in grade school together. A year later they were married.

A security guard watching the old man with the faraway look stopped Granddad and asked if everything was OK. Granddad shook the man's hand and asked what time it was. A lady behind the candy counter told him it was a little after nine. Granddad went to the candy counter and bought a box of chocolate-covered caramels just like he had on that day long ago. He told the candy lady to never get old. Then he gave a caramel to the security guard and revolved out onto the sidewalk and back into 1966.

People were walking along with business concerns and tired faces. He gave the caramels to strangers as he walked to the car. Some ate them. Some took them, but later tossed them into the street thinking Granddad was crazy. When the box was empty, he set it on top of Cutlass, got out his keys, and drove away. The box fell in a puddle and wilted in on itself. It was drizzling, so he flipped on the windshield wipers. He turned on the radio, twisted the dial away from the old people's station and tuned into the youth station, KXOK. The announcer was talking about the Beatles. Granddad listened and drove the wrong way down a one-way street.

++++

Patrick sat in a stuffed antique chair at the funeral parlor. The parlor was in a Victorian home that smelled like graham crackers and burnt coffee. In front of him, he could see the stalks of relatives standing and visiting. Beyond the relatives, he could see Nana's face in the open casket. She came in and out of view as the living relatives shifted and gestured.

"Then I spotted blood in my urine," said one of Dad's cousins. It was Cousin Jack, a relative who came around for funerals. He was standing by the casket talking to some men about his kidney stones. "It hurt like hell when they passed," he said. Earlier Jack had handed out pens from his construction materials sales job. The pens read: *I am a friend of Jack Hoff.* He had given one to Patrick. Patrick put it in his pocket.

Patrick caught glimpses of Nana and remembered her life. He thought of the dollar bills in the birthday cards, the way she safety-pinned Granddad's pajamas on him so they would fit when he spent the night. And he thought about the last time he saw her. She had offered to help him go to the Monday Club with Ebby. "Be good," she had told him before the robbery.

He blamed himself for her death. If he hadn't robbed Ben Franklin, Nana would probably still be alive. She would have set him up with Ebby through the Monday Club. And everything would have been great. Instead, she was dead, he was on probation and would probably end up in prison someday, maybe the electric chair.

Someone sat down on the love seat near Patrick. He looked over. It was Sister Jenny. She was wearing her white habit again and eating a graham cracker from one of the dishes. It was her first appearance in public since the Easter Sunday vomiting incident at the Two Love Birds restaurant.

"Hello, Patrick."

"Hi, Sister."

"I'm sorry about your Nana. She was a good Nana. She loved you boys very much."

"Yeah." Patrick looked toward the casket. Some relatives were standing in the way. Cousin Jack was greeting another family member loudly. "Len, you son of gun, where's all your hair?"

Patrick looked over at Sister Jenny. He looked at her face. It was fuller. She looked healthier and scrubbed. When she blinked Patrick stole a glance at her habit to check for vomit stains. Her habit looked cleaner, but maybe a little off-white from the experience.

"I heard about what happened at the Ben Franklin," she said.

Patrick looked at his funeral shoes.

"I know how it is sometimes," she whispered, "You just got into some trouble. But don't let it mark you, Patrick. Somehow … we all have to conquer ourselves and try to recover lost ground."

Cousin Jack pulled up his pant leg to show some men a scar he got from jumping off a tire swing into the Meramec River. He had been drinking Stag beer in the can that day and landed on a submerged rock. The scar ran up his calf. "It's permanent," he told them. "I'll go to my grave with it."

Sister Jenny put her hand on Patrick's shoulder to say more, but the funeral home man pressed a button on the easy play organ. A somber, attention-grabbing chord throbbed through the room. Everyone hushed. Granddad walked in. Dad walked over to him.

"Pop, we tried to phone you this morning, but there was no answer. *Are you all right?*"

Granddad hugged his son for the first time since the Cardinals won the pennant in 1946. They looked at each other, father and son, but before they could speak, a frenzied woman ran up.

It was Nana's sister from New Orleans, old Aunt Genevieve, with the liver spots on her arms and cigarettes on her breath. "Oh, Joe," she said clutching Granddad's suit sleeve, "This is a short deal we've got here, a short deal." She broke into a coughing jag and went off to the side to clear out her lungs.

The funeral home man pressed some more buttons to make minor chords shake the drapes. Everyone stood toward the front of the room by the casket, and it got quiet. Monsignor O'Day appeared in a black cassock with a white smock embroidered with a gold cross. He stood by the casket. He led everyone in saying the Our Father and Hail Mary. The crowd stood facing Nana and prayed along. Patrick listened to all the adult voices saying the familiar words. It was like hearing the Pledge of Allegiance or the alphabet recited. For the first time everyone in the room was saying the same words at the same time. Everyone could hear each other and look at Nana and let the words move in their mouths while their minds wandered. Monsignor said the words over and over. Our Fathers, Hail Marys—he issued prayers like first-class postage stamps for an important package of unknown weight. Then he stopped, and the room was quiet.

The funeral home man stepped forward. "You may now walk past the deceased to pay your final respects before we leave for the church," he told the crowd.

The mourners filed by—about sixty people—friends, neighbors, cousins, in-laws, three grandchildren, one son and one husband. The line moved along too fast for long goodbyes. Mom and Dad went by. Then came Aunt Genevieve crying. Then, finally, the last one was Granddad. He stood alone by her. The room was quiet. The funeral home man looked at Dad. Dad put his hand on Granddad's shoulder. The funeral home man started to close the lid. Granddad slid his hand toward the gap, as if he was trying to stop an elevator door from closing. They paused for him to look at her. Dad whispered something to Granddad and nodded to the funeral home man. The lid slowly closed. Patrick saw Nana for the last time—her face puffy and stiff. He decided he would try to be good and recover lost ground like Sister Jenny said.

- chapter twenty-four -

THE BEATLES HAD WRITTEN LOVE LETTERS. The letters were set to music. The music was pressed onto vinyl and sent out all over the world. In Webster Groves girls received them and shut their bedroom doors to be alone and open their love letters. They dipped the needle on the spinning record and the words poured out of the speaker. The girls lay on their beds looking into John, Paul, George and Ringo's eyes on the album covers. The girls felt the new thing. They tried to choose which Beatle to love the most, sometimes changing partners in mid song, while the Beatles sang to each of them personally. Nobody around town had ever loved them so beautifully. Parents, not understanding, yelled up for the girls to *please shut off that racket.* What made it even worse was the fact that the Beatles never phoned. They were as near as the record player, but as far away as England. They said they loved each girl. Yet each girl had only pictures and songs. Then the impossible happened. The Beatles came for a visit.

On a rainy night in August 1966, the Beatles performed at Busch Stadium in downtown St. Louis. Thousands of girls paid four-dollars-and-fifty-cents each to see up close and personal the ones who had loved them so much from afar.

Granddad circled the stadium in the Cutlass Supreme looking for a parking space. John, Patrick and Teddy were with him. They were supposed to be at his house "spending a quiet night" to cheer him up after the funeral. But at the last minute he said, "Hell, let's go for a ride." When they got downtown, John saw the crowds and the police.

"Oh, Granddad, can we go? Can we, please?" John said.

"Boys, this is a short deal we've got here. Tonight we're all young."

Granddad honked as a group of protesters crossed the street in front of him. They carried a sign reading "God Forever, the Beatles Never."

"Out of the way, you hooligans, we just came from a funeral," Granddad yelled.

They parked the car and zipped up their coats. Granddad opened an umbrella and picked up Teddy. Teddy recognized the baseball stadium from a past trip with Dad. "Are we going to a Cardinals game?" he asked. Granddad bought the tickets and they went through the turnstile. He wiped the rain off their seats with a handkerchief and they sat down. Teenagers talked and smoked and paid no attention to the opening act already in progress.

"Is *this* the Beatles?" Granddad asked.

"No," John said.

"Well, who's this?" Granddad said.

"I don't know," John said.

A teenage boy behind Granddad tapped him on the shoulder. "This band is called The Remains. It's The Remains, man."

"The Remains," Granddad mumbled. He looked at his grandsons seated with him and looked around at the thousands of young people. He realized this was their 1925. He got out a cigar.

"Hey, man, don't light that dog turd," the teenager behind him said.

Granddad reeled around to vent on the youth. But the teenager smiled and offered Granddad a small, hand-rolled cigarette. Granddad put away his cigar. He puffed on the lively blend and relaxed. He watched some girls in tie-dye shirts unfurl a banner from a box seat by the first base line: HAPPINESS IS THE BEATLES.

At nine o'clock an announcer took the stage. This was it. Everyone stood and started applauding and cheering. The announcer said something. But no one could hear him over the screaming. Then the flashcubes started going off. The Beatles ran onto the field from the Cardinal's dugout. Granddad picked up Teddy. John and Patrick stood on their seats. The flashcubes lit up the stadium like the sun was shining. The Beatles ran through the rain. They plugged in their guitars. They smiled and waved. They wore double-vested suits with white shirts, but no ties. Ringo wore a plaid hat. He started drumming. Faint singing could be heard through the screams.

It was the song "Rock and Roll Music."

Teenagers danced in the stands and shook their long haircuts. Granddad clapped along reluctantly. It was foolishness, he knew, but it was better than sitting at home writing funeral thank you cards. He watched his grandkids enjoy themselves. He smoked some more of the cigarette being passed to him and smiled at the kids around him who smiled back. They may be foolish, but they were good kids, happy. *Alive.* Then, feeling buoyant, he drifted into the aisle to dance a 1920s step with two sixteen-year old girls. They had never known anyone so old who liked the Beatles. They took Granddad's outstretched hands and flung their blue-jeaned hips left and right. The rain came down. The Beatles kept singing love songs and the crowd kept screaming.

They sang "She's a Woman." Patrick didn't know the words, but he clapped along. His brother John danced and sang along in an English accent. Teddy joined the commotion, but kept glancing at the dugout to see when the Cardinals would take the field. The flashcubes and screaming and the strains of the day churned in Granddad's mind. He raised his eyebrows and looked out over the crowd. He wiped his hand across his wet forehead and tried to forget that he was old and that it was 1966. He was surrounded by young people, by music, dancing, and cooling rain. Then he felt it. Whatever he had once felt in the Famous Barr revolving door—whatever Patrick had felt in school sitting across from Ebby—whatever anyone feels the first time.

Granddad felt the new thing. This time he felt it for no one in particular. He felt it for *life.*

As the Beatles started into "Day Tripper," Granddad floated down the aisle shaking hands with strangers. He leaned in toward their ears to shout that they "represent a fine generation." He handed out cigars. He danced with more young ladies by the box seats. Then with a short hop, he was onto the playing field. He danced in big circles. He waved his arms to the crowd. The adulating flashcubes and shining rain embraced him. He started to cry. He told the crowd he loved them. He told them to stay young. He shouted to them that love was the best thing in life, "better than real estate." He skipped in circles. The Beatles kept playing. Ringo saw Granddad and smiled. Granddad smiled back. The crowd cheered, and the St. Louis Police rushed onto the field and arrested him.

fall

- chapter twenty-five -

PATRICK KNOTTED HIS NAVY BLUE uniform necktie and came downstairs for another school day. In the front hallway he exchanged glances with the photo gallery of the living and the dead. He saw Mom's father, Patrick Senior. He saw the strong, but sad eyes of Sister Jenny reminding him to be good. And there was a picture of Nana with a purgatory prayer card stuck in the frame. Patrick stepped out the front door to get the *Globe Democrat* off the front lawn. It was still dark and cold enough to see his breath. Most of the leaves had already fallen. The Pevely milk truck pulled up. The milkman looked tired from getting to the dairy at four in the morning. He gave Patrick a bottle of milk. "Stay in school," the milkman said. Patrick grabbed the paper and squeezed it to slip off the string. He opened the front door and tossed the string to the side in the mud. It landed in a pile of strings that showed him he was climbing the seven-story mountain of getting the paper every day and staying out of trouble.

In the kitchen Mom was standing by the stove in her bathrobe. She was eight months pregnant. She cut sandwiches in triangle halves on the porcelain counter top of the Hoosier cabinet. The dog waited for scraps between her fleece-lined slippers. The little radio above the kitchen sink was tuned to KMOX, which was a playing the morning march. This morning it was John Phillip Sousa. Coffee shot up and burbled down through the clear top of the percolator. He put the milk bottle on the counter, and Mom hugged him.

"I ironed your Cub Scout uniform and put it in a paper bag for your field trip today," she said.

"OK."

"*OK?* Whatever happened to thanks?"

"Thanks, Mom."

"Where is your field trip?"

"I don't know. I forgot," he said, tired.

She tossed a scrap to the dog and folded the waxed paper around the sandwiches. "You forgot? I guess you'd rather be walking home with Ebby than be a Cub Scout."

Sousa notes roared. He fumbled the *Globe Democrat* and it fell to the floor. He picked it up quickly. To hear Ebby's name spoken so suddenly—and accurately—left him flustered. Ebby was not a name to be flicked around the room like dog scraps. It was much more than a name. It was jumping in front of the train together. It was hearing her lie while he hid in the creek to protect him from the Special Agent. Ebby was the only girl who ever made him feel the new thing.

Mom snapped open two brown paper lunch bags. "Well, how come I never hear you talk about her? We practically had an Ebby alert last spring. Ebby, Ebby, Ebby … I thought you liked her. Isn't she the one who called you on the phone?"

He lowered his voice. "Yeah."

She put the sandwiches in the bags. "You still like her?" Mom said, raising her voice above the Sousa march.

He looked to see if anybody else was listening. Dad, John and Teddy were out in the breakfast room. *The Lone Ranger* was on the black and white TV. He looked at Mom, then nodded a secretive yes.

She petted his hair. "Patrick, it's nothing to be ashamed of. I think it's a good thing to have a girlfriend. You'll have lots of girlfriends. It's why God made Adam and Eve. It's what makes the world go round. Someday you'll grow up and marry a girl like Ebby and raise a Catholic family. You two still get together?"

Still get together? The way she said it angered him, as if Ebby was just another date like the many she had at the Parkmoor before she met Dad. He looked at the dog. "No."

"Why not?"

"We're not in the same class anymore."

Mom opened a drawer to the Hoosier cabinet and got out a busted black crayon. "Why not?"

"She's in the other second grade class."

Mom wrote "John" and "Patrick" and "Teddy" on the lunch bags. "Well, that'll happen. Jimmy Purvis isn't in your class anymore either. But you still walk to school with him. Can't you walk with Ebby?"

"She gets a ride now that it's cold."

"I see. Well, why don't you call her up after school? Go walk the dog with her?"

"Mom, I can't just *call her*," he said as the Sousa march on the radio fired its final trumpet blasts. "I'm too—"

"Shy?"

The kitchen got quiet, as an announcer began reading the opening hog report. Patrick looked in the breakfast room to see if anyone was listening. They were still watching *The Lone Ranger*. Mom put some toast in the toaster with one hand on her back to ease a baby kick.

"Patrick, there's nothing to be shy about. Girls are just people. You must get that from your father. He's not very good at talking to girls, either, even me. It's probably because he was an only child with no sisters. He's like all the men in that family. Nana used to complain that they'd go up to Davenport to visit Great Grandpa Cantwell, and all the men would ignore the women. They'd just sit around with their spittoons and cigars and talk about nothing but baseball and real estate. Maybe that's why you're shy. It's a family trait. Sometimes when I'm reading James Bond, I wonder if all men are like your father."

Patrick got a bad feeling that Kurt Logan was right. "Mom, are you and Dad going to get divorced someday?"

She looked at him. "Patrick! What makes you say such a thing? "

"Kurt Logan."

"Well, don't you listen to him. Hmmph. *Kurt Logan!* Your Dad would never divorce me or run away from us. *He's a very good Dad.* It's just that he doesn't show his love by hugging and kissing. He shows it by ... by getting in that Falcon and driving downtown every morning."

Dad called in from the breakfast room. "Hey, Patrick, have you got the sports section?"

She hugged Patrick. He kissed her fast on the cheek, so no one would notice.

"I'm going to keep that all day. Now, get some cereal. And maybe you'll see Ebby today. Maybe you can do something nice for her, too."

Patrick went into the breakfast room and gave Dad the paper.

"Thanks," Dad said.

John and Teddy were daydreaming over bowls of Sugar Pops. The yellow cereal box, featuring a cowboy with a bull whip, was strategically positioned between the boys as a bad breath stopper. Dad was eating All Bran and sipping a glass of prune juice, as he pulled out the sports section. Teddy saw the sports page and his eyes brightened. He was in kindergarten now, and showing a keen interest in sports.

"Dad, what's happening with the Cardinals?" Teddy said. Dad didn't hear him. He was reading about the Football Cardinals' latest loss. Teddy tapped on the sports page. "Dad, did the Cardinals win?" Dad lowered the paper and took a spoonful of All Bran. He looked fondly at Teddy. Teddy was his only son showing a wholesome, character-building interest in sports. John and Patrick—the ones on probation for robbing the Ben Franklin—sat staring at a *Godzilla* commercial.

"No, Teddy, the Cardinals lost. But they signed a new quarterback ... Ringo Starr," Dad said.

John turned away from the TV. Dad quickly pretended to read the paper. "What about Ringo?" John said.

"Oh, nothing, nothing you wouldn't know yourself if you showed an interest in reading the paper in the morning. You two boys know how to read? What are those nuns teaching you? Why don't you ever want to read the sports page ... or at least the front page?"

John and Patrick looked at each other, then at the front page. It was lying there by the glass of prune juice. A headline said something about President Johnson and more troops. Another article was about a single engine plane crash. They wondered what it meant. But then they turned back to the TV. The Winchell-Mahoney ventriloquist show was on.

"IT'S WINCHELL-MAHONEY TIME...."

The theme music transported them to a wooden dummy kingdom where no one ever had to work downtown, go to school, or get killed. They munched Sugar Pops in rhythm with the song and waited for the appearance of their hero, Knucklehead Smith.

Someone knocked at the back door, and they all turned to look. It was Jimmy Purvis. He was dressed in his school uniform and tie. Steam gathered on the windowpane in front of his runny nose and his new front tooth. Jimmy had a complete smile again. The dog barked and Mom went to the back door to let him in.

"*Why Jimmy!* Did your parents let you leave the house *without a coat?*"

Mom said.

"It's not cold," Jimmy said.

"Good morning, Jimmy," everyone mumbled—everyone except Teddy. Teddy stirred the yellow dregs of his Sugar Pops milk and looked at the heater. Teddy didn't like Jimmy because every morning, he let in a blast of cold air, then sat in front of the heater, blocking the warm air.

"*Jayzul,* it's colder than blazes out there," Dad said to Jimmy, "Quick, sit on the heater and warm up."

Jimmy sat on the heater.

"How are your folks?" Dad said, glancing at the sports page and the Winchell-Mahoney show.

"Oh fine," Jimmy said watching TV, "My older brother got accepted at the Jesuit high school." Dad put down the paper and looked at Jimmy. "But it's expensive as heck," Jimmy said, "Now, my parents are arguing over whether they can afford it."

Dad opened his mouth to ask *how expensive.* But before he could speak, Mom blurted in from the kitchen. "That's wonderful! A Jesuit high school! Everyone at Bridge Club says there's nothing like a Jesuit education to refine boys, keep them out of trouble, and get them ready for college."

Dad frowned. He looked at his watch and wondered what it would cost to send his own sons to a Jesuit high school. "If you ask me, those Jevies have a racket going. We're already paying property taxes through the nose. When I was a boy we went to *public* schools. Webster High! The Statesmen!" Memories of malt shop dates, bonfires and Turkey Day games swept through his mind. "How'd you boys like to wear the orange and black someday?"

Before they could answer, Mom called in from the kitchen. "Jimmy, are you all excited about you and Patrick making your first confession and first communion this week?"

But Jimmy Purvis didn't hear her. No one did. They were all watching the grand entrance of Knucklehead Smith. A wooden dummy with buck-teeth, Knucklehead wore a black-and-white checkered suit and polka-dot tie. Unprepared for life, and totally lacking in Jesuit refinement, he spoke in a mumbling, confused voice that everyone loved. He tossed a whipped cream pie at his fellow dummy, Jerry Mahoney. Dad laughed. All the boys laughed. Mom brought Dad his coffee and watched her men. She smiled. Mom didn't ask any more questions. The boys didn't care about Jesuit high school, or first confession, or more troops in Vietnam, or single engine plane crashes. Everyone

119

knew that sort of thing was out there waiting. In a few minutes dishes would fly to the sink. Teeth would have to be scrubbed. Dad would drive downtown. The boys would walk to school. Mom would descend the basement steps to the laundry room. The troubles of the day were waiting. It was best now not to stir up such things. Dad drank his prune juice and winced. These were the last precious moments of Winchell-Mahoney Time.

- chapter twenty-six -

JIMMY PURVIS SHIVERED as the boys walked to school. They hopped over the back fence and cut through a yard by the creek. They walked along the sidewalk as a Bi-State bus dropped off a black woman from north St. Louis to clean a Webster Groves house for ten-dollars a day. She was heavy-set and bundled up. She said *good morning* to the boys. They said *hi* back and Patrick asked, *how are you?* "Highly favored and surely blessed," she said. Then she looked Jimmy up and down and scolded him for not wearing a coat.

They walked past the grassy median where Jimmy had once picked dandelions. Now, the dandelions were dead and gone. Beneath the train bridge, pigeons huddled in the upper nooks to keep warm. The embankment alongside the bridge was still black from the fire. No one said anything about the tracks anymore. They walked along. They had avoided even the topic of the tracks ever since they went on probation. Jimmy talked with Teddy about hockey.

"We need an NHL team, but we'll never get one, because we're too far south," Jimmy said. Teddy nodded. Then Jimmy lectured on driveway hockey. He explained how you play with an orange plastic puck full of bb's. "It's hard to do a rising slap shot, but I've got it down," Jimmy said. Jimmy was boring everyone but Teddy with the story about how his wooden stick broke, but he saved it by putting a plastic extender on the end that he held over a hot stove to curve it. Teddy was nodding and feeling alive. To think, a second grader was honoring him with a sports seminar.

But John and Patrick hated sports. To them sports was a waste of time. One team wins. One team loses. It's all pointless, John would say. *Who gives a crap?*

John was visualizing the finger positions for a G 13th guitar chord. Patrick was secretly watching for a glance of Ebby going by in her family Cadillac. Hers was a fast Cadillac that never honked hello and the windows were hard to see in. Today she must have been dropped off already, because Patrick didn't see her car.

When the gold statute of Mary Queen of Our Hearts rose above the treetops, they broke into a run. Teddy ran straight for the kindergarten house. John headed for the dumpster where Kurt Logan loitered until the last bell. Jimmy was freezing, so he and Patrick ducked in the church to get warm. They stood in a small entrance hallway where a heater was blowing. It was a marble, echoey hallway. There was an outer door and an inner door. In between was private. Beyond the inner door old people who were getting close to death seemed to be racking up points by attending daily Mass. Jimmy shivered and rubbed his hands in the heat.

"Why *don't* you wear a coat?" Patrick whispered.

Jimmy looked at Patrick and tried to decide whether to tell him. They were pretty good friends. They had hopped trains, been arrested together, and seen each other poop in the scrub brush near the tracks. So he told him. "I just can't stand my coat. I hide it in the bushes as soon as I'm out of the yard. It makes me look like such a *roofus*. It's the same kind of coat that those twins wear, the ones that get straight A's," Jimmy said.

"Oh, that's bad. The same kind?"

"Exact same."

"Can't your mom return it?"

"No, I shot it with the bb gun. It's full of holes. I was so pissed. No girl would look at me in that thing." Then he added with intrigue, "I guess you know about me and Cindy."

"What?"

"That's right, you weren't at the Halloween party. What did you do Halloween anyway?"

Patrick got out his new scout knife, hoping its coolness would offset what he was about to say. "Went with Dad on our block only. He brought a flashlight."

"Roofus!"

"I know," Patrick said, opening the blade and dragging it across the metal strips of the heat vent. "What about Cindy?"

"Cindy, Cindy, Cindy ... God, I love her. We're going to the carnival tonight." Jimmy snorted up his snot and fingered back his hair at the thought of Cindy.

Patrick ran the words through his mind again—*going to the carnival.* He looked at Jimmy. "So? Everybody's going. The whole school's going."

Jimmy shook his head. "I don't mean we're *going.* I mean we're *going. Together.* It's like *a date.*"

Patrick unzipped his coat. It was getting warm. Father Maligan and the old people at Mass were grunting out hallelujahs behind the door. He looked at Jimmy.

"A date?"

"Yeah."

Patrick put down his bag containing his Cub Scout uniform. He put away his knife. Jimmy looked at him.

"Look at you, fooling around with scouts, showing off that knife. Where'd you get that thing?"

"My Mom. It was her Dad's knife. He was—"

"Yeah, *I know,* he was an Eagle Scout. You're not Eagle Scout material. Face it. You need to get going with the times. *Scouts! Hmmph,* get going with some girl. What about that Ebby?"

"Who?"

"You know, that girl in my class. I thought last year you *loved* her."

"Loved her? Ebby?" He reached to pick his nose under the pressure, but caught himself. "Jimmy, there were so many girls in my class. I—"

"Oh, well, I guess I'm just advanced. You've got to have that *feeling* before you date … that confidence. My dad's a salesman. He tells us all the time at dinner the secret is you have to sell yourself. And have confidence. So, I faked it. At the party she was standing by herself dancing to some record. I said, *Hi, Cindy, you want to dance?* No one had ever danced with a girl like that before. No other boy even *thinks* about dancing with girls. Like I said, I must be advanced. So, I took her hands and we kind of went in circles in the hall. It was like no other feeling in the world. Then I bumped into the dehumidifier. *Water everywhere!* Man, but I asked her. *Hey, Cindy, you want to go with me to the mission carnival?* And she just looked at me and said, *OK.*"

Patrick stood there listening to the heater blow and the nasally singing of Father Maligan. Then Jimmy added, "There's just one thing I'm worried about tonight."

"What?"

"You think I'll need a coat?"

The communion song was playing, signaling the end of Mass. A lady who had just swallowed a host opened the door to leave. She was startled to see two boys in the foyer. She stomped her boots and looked at them. Her cheeks had lots of makeup. Black eyebrow liner was dashed across her eyebrows like a poorly painted monster model. "Boys, what are you doing here?"

"Getting warm," Patrick said.

She whipped on her gloves and delivered a whispered sermon. The words shot over the coffee stains on her lower teeth. "Boys, look at yourselves! How can you be standing out here... *when God is right in there on the other side of that door?* Don't you want to go in and spend time with him?" They looked at each other and looked at the door she was talking about. It was heavy oak. But before they could think up an excuse, she left. They peeked outside and saw her marching away in the cold. She went past the flagpole. At the bottom of the flagpole a nun waved to her. The nun was helping four kindergarteners pull up the American flag. Patrick and Jimmy ran out of the church into the school.

- chapter twenty-seven -

AT EIGHT O'CLOCK the principal, a nun wearing the modern-style habit, laid aside a *Reader's Digest* article on delinquent boys and grabbed the microphone. She flipped a switch on the humming tube control panel. Wall speakers in classrooms throughout the school were activated. On the speaker in Patrick's second-grade class, the cherry red light blinked on. Students hushed. The principal's progressive, but authoritative voice echoed through the school.

"Good morning, students...."

On the front lawn, the janitor was half-asleep, picking up gum wrappers when the voices of six-hundred students throbbed from the classroom windows.

"GOOD MORNING, PRINCIPAL."

The janitor flinched. The principal smiled slightly as she paced about her office, checking the bookcase for dust. She felt the building vibrate and looked at the nearby picture of her married sister in Kansas City who had only five children. She continued with the official news of the day:

"Today is Wednesday, November 2nd, All Souls Day. I hope you all got a lot of candy for Halloween. Today is also Sandy Mullenbrock's tenth birthday, grade five...."

Patrick sat at his desk and listened. He looked at the windows. Halloween decorations were taped to the glass, orange construction paper pumpkins and black witches. His teacher, Sister Mathilda, was the only nun still wearing the old-fashioned black and white habit. She was short and stooped over with a clean, wrinkled face and a double chin like a turkey wattle. An eighty-seven-year old, Sister Mathilda never heard anything worth her time on morning announcements.

Every morning when the red light came on and the modern voice of the forty-year old principal invaded her room, Sister Mathilda would sing softly a Latin Mass hymn from the good old days, the days of wooden kneelers—before they had vinyl cushions. Humming to herself while she passed out papers, she redeemed the time the announcements wasted. Time was the thing. Not much left. Retirement lurked at each parish banquet. Nuns she once knew were now dead. Soon her time would come. And when asked to give account, instead of having everything swept and tidy, and her students prepared for this world and the next, she was surrounded by chaos and mediocrity. There was Vatican Two, the vote to eliminate traditional habits, a general casualness about having a soul, and declining penmanship. The principal continued.

"On a serious note, today is the last day to guess how many M and M's are in the glass jar. It's also the final day of our mission drive."

In Patrick's class some students started getting out money to donate. A girl dropped a quarter on the floor. It rolled near the trash can. The girl raised her hand. Sister Mathilda, who had cataracts, could not see the quarter. But she heard it. She gave a general order in the direction of the disturbance. "You may pick it up."

The principal continued, "The mission carnival is tonight in the gym. Money raised will benefit Catholic charities in forty-seven countries worldwide. There will be games and booths and prizes. We hope you'll bring a loved one. Now please rise."

Patrick stood up and put his hand on his heart. He pictured Ebby down in her classroom doing the same. He said the Pledge of Allegiance. Then the principal led everyone in a Hail Mary. Patrick said the words and watched the steam leak out of the knob of the radiator. Above the radiator the windows with the black witches were fogging up. Outside the window, old people leaving Mass were shaking hands and limping toward their cars. On top of the church the gold statue of Mary stood with arms outstretched against the November clouds.

The announcements ended.

"Let's get out those Number Two pencils," Sister Mathilda said. She shut the hallway door and pulled down the door shade. The classroom was hers. No more wasted time. "I've got a special assignment for you today. We're going back in time to the McGuffey Reader. If you'll look at the paper I passed out...." Patrick looked at his. It was a copy of fancy handwriting, the kind Sister

Mathilda had learned in a one-room schoolhouse when Teddy Roosevelt was President.

Sister Mathilda had made copies in the faculty lounge early that morning—before any of the other teachers had arrived. She didn't want another meeting with the principal about retiring the McGuffey Reader. Operating the modern mimeograph machine was her only problem. It was almost as mysterious to her as the Cutlass Supreme she had won in the raffle. The Cutlass she kept parked as a bargaining chip against forced retirement. But the mimeograph machine she drove. It was a hot rod to help young minds. The spinning blue ink cylinder was a blur to her, and measuring out the ink was hard. So with no one looking, she just dumped in a few glugs. Fumes like rubbing alcohol rose from each page. Patrick put the paper to his nose and inhaled. Other students did the same. Sister Mathilda tightened her habit belt.

"Handwriting can be exhilarating. Let's begin by practicing capital letters for Q, R, S, T, U, V," she said. "Try to make them look perfect."

The girl who had dropped her quarter raised her hand. Sister Mathilda saw a vague stalk waving in the air.

"Yes?"

"Sister, did you forget something? You're supposed to—"

"No, I didn't forget. I'll collect your carnival money while you get started."

Papers rustled as the class of thirty-five students leaned into the assignment. They were resigned to it like prisoners of war building a bridge deep in some steamy hot jungle. It was a lot of work. Frail hands got writer's cramp. Some asked for water. But Sister Mathilda said no. If she let one get water, then she would have to let another, and another. Everyone wanted to escape, go to recess. Patrick thought of Ebby, and tolerated handwriting only by associating it with the beautiful handwritten name he had seen her write in first grade.

Sister Mathilda sat in her metal desk chair and sighed. She opened a drawer and pulled out a coffee can. Her desk was arranged with Helen Keller efficiency. Everything in its place. That way any official visitor—the Monsignor or Principal—could see by her swift precision of movement that the modern cataract surgery was unnecessary. She put the Old Judge can on her desktop and closed the drawer. She noticed the recess bell was too close to the edge. She adjusted it. She looked at her desk calendar. November 2nd, All Souls Day. The words burned through the blear of her cataracts. From deep within the school basement, the furnace made the radiators bang, as she remembered the old days. Before mission carnivals. Before modern announcements. Back when

All Souls Day was observed. Back then the living went to church throughout the day to pray for the dead. It was the one day of the year when a quick Our Father and Hail Mary could turn the key and get souls out of purgatory and into heaven.

She got a chill and turned up the radiator.

"Children," she said turning the heat up all the way, "while you practice your handwriting, I'm going to collect your mission money and tell you about a place. It's a very bad room where people are forced to work. It's hot and there is no fun and they all want to leave. Can you imagine such a place?"

The radiators seethed. Steam thickened on the windows. The paper witches flapped in the rising heat. Potent fumes from the mimeograph ink collided in the atmosphere, forming new volatile compounds. Sister Mathilda's ghostly voice drifted over the desks. Nickels, dimes and quarters clinked into the coffee can. She paused by Patrick. She looked down on him. He kept writing.

"Patrick."

"Yes."

"Your S's have potential."

"Thank you."

She continued, holding the coffee can left and right as she walked up the rows. "Today is All Souls Day. It's the only day all year you can help those people get out of that room. If you go to the church today and say an Our Father and Hail Mary for someone, a soul will get lifted out of purgatory and go to heaven."

The temperature was rising. The spit dried up in Patrick's mouth. He leaned to one side, as far as he could from the radiators.

"Pray for your dead relatives. If you don't have any yet, pray for the Most Forgotten Soul in purgatory. He's down there. Right now. He's been down there … suffering for maybe hundreds of years, lifting heavy rocks, clothes all torn, flames along the path, suffering every day with no water or relatives up here who even know his name anymore. What a difference you could make in his day."

She held the can out to the last student up front. The boy stood up. Everyone looked at him. He got out his wallet and put a dollar in the can. Sister Mathilda smiled. He sat down. Children stopped writing to ponder what a dollar might have bought: cool lemon drinks, frozen Heath Bars, Drumsticks....

"Someday, that person you help release today … he'll be there for your judgment day to put in a good word for you."

She put the coffee can on the desk of a girl in the front row. It was Cindy, the girl Jimmy Purvis had asked to the mission carnival. Cindy was a nice girl. Cindy was a pretty girl. She never did anything wrong. Cindy smiled at Sister Mathilda. Sister Mathilda touched her soft, young cheek.

"Cindy, would you please take this money down to the gym and put it with the rest of the mission money?"

"Yes, sister."

Sister Mathilda turned to walk away. She stepped toward her desk. The room temperature had risen to eighty-six degrees. Sweat trickled down Patrick's back. He rubbed his eyes. He opened them. He thought he saw an apparition near Cindy. It was a bright form, a bridge of autumn colors in the air between the two rows of desks. It seemed solid, permanent, and beautiful. He blinked. It was gone. He heard a splash. Something was dripping off Cindy. Projectile vomit—the worst kind. The boy across the row had turned his head and launched an arch of barf all over her.

- chapter twenty-eight -

THE JANITOR MOVED QUICKLY from years of practice. He bolted from the boiler room leaving behind a bouncing basketball that he had been patching when the vomit alarm sounded by his workbench. Patrick opened the window. Cool air rushed in as the janitor jogged in carrying a broom, a special flip-top dustpan and a canister of sawdust.

"Over here!" Sister Mathilda directed. She was standing by the abandoned desks with Cindy dripping in the center. Cindy stood as still as a statue, whimpering. The janitor patted her back.

"There, there, now, honey … Did you get it all up?"

"No, it wasn't her. It was him," Sister Mathilda said, pointing to the blur of a puffy boy across from Cindy. He was breathing easier now with a deep, satisfied look on his face. The janitor wiped off Cindy with a shop rag.

"That's good enough," Sister Mathilda said, "I think both of you two better go to the nurse's office. Anyone else feeling sick?"

Students watching from the sidelines gulped down air from the open windows. Cindy and the sick boy left. The janitor began sprinkling sawdust on the scene. The sawdust fell like manna. It was a specially formulated sawdust made at a remote convent in Knob Noster, Missouri. The nuns there, stout and wearing protective masks, operated heavy machinery to pulverize dead trees. The fine wood powder was then sprayed with a bile-neutralizing chemical—X-33. It had been developed by a Catholic physicist on retreat. Schools across the Midwest ordered half a million dollars worth every year. All proceeds benefited Catholic charities worldwide.

"I'll have this cleaned up in a jiff, Sister."

"Hope you don't get sick. There must be a flu bug."

He covered his mouth with a face mask, then wiped off the sides of the coffee can and handed it to Sister Mathilda. She turned and called the first student she saw.

"Patrick, take this down to the gym and put it with the rest of the mission money."

"Who, me?"

++++

Patrick carried the money toward the gym. He saw the hallway door to the gym open. Some other kids who had already dumped their class's money walked out of the gym and down the hall. He went through the door and climbed the steps onto the stage. On the stage was a crucifix, looming over a wooden chest for the mission money. He looked around. He could see the gym floor below.

Balloons, game booths and crepe paper waited for the evening mission carnival. It was quiet. He opened the treasure chest lid. Thousands of coins sparkled in the stage light. More coins than he had ever seen—more coins than at the St. Louis Art Museum wishing well under the green water. And it wasn't just coins. Swimming throughout was currency—green dollar bills, five spots, even a ten-dollar bill—begging like forgotten souls to be lifted upward. Patrick looked at it all. He pretended he was a bank robber and grabbed a fistful and squeezed it. He wished he had one of Jimmy's dad's Winstons in his mouth like a real bank robber, not to light, just to steady his nerves during the holdup. The coins pressed into his palm. The currency felt right. He looked around. No one was watching. The money was destined for Catholic charities in forty-seven countries worldwide. Taking a little wouldn't hurt. Maybe a few village people might have to skip custard pie. He deserved that much—at least what was in his grip. It was as good as his. It just needed a quick trip to his pocket. He looked around. All clear.

But he remembered the Ben Franklin incident, and probation, and Sister Jenny telling him to recover lost ground. He knew he couldn't really steal the money. He flicked it loose. It fell with the rest of the coins and bills. He emptied the Old Judge coffee can into the pile and left the stage defeated. It was a shameful thing to have pretended stealing the money because he realized his heart was ready to steal again, even though his mind knew it was wrong.

Opening the door to the hallway, he noticed somebody was coming. He reversed back behind the door and looked through the crack. Way down the hall, three students approached carrying more mission money. One of them was Ebby. It had been days since he had seen her. She looked great. Her skin still had a summer tan compared to the other students. The talk around recess was her parents had taken her on a jet to Florida. Patrick had never been on a plane. He had been to the Belleville flea market once with Dad in the Falcon. She was getting closer. Her plaid skirt swayed past the used book table. She wore green socks. They were pulled up just below her knees. Her shoe tassels flapped stylishly, and she looked ready to dance. Her hair shined and she flipped it over her shoulders as she passed the bone-white statue of John the Baptist. Patrick could hear the mission pennies jingling in her jar. She held the jar in one hand, while her free hand played imaginary piano notes at her side. She was coming. Patrick looked around. He ran back up on the stage and hid behind the curtain.

It was dark at the back of the stage. Patrick could make out the forms of theatrical props—a life-sized Santa, a giant bumblebee, and a plywood balcony from the Romeo and Juliet production. He breathed quietly and peeked through a crack in the burgundy curtain. Ebby and the two other students came up on the stage. Their feet were like soldiers on the hardwood floor. The oldest boy, a sixth-grade Boy Scout, flipped open the lid to the treasure box.

"Look at all this money!" he said.

"It's a shame to give it to the poor," the younger boy said.

Get right! the older boy said, smacking him across the head. Ebby didn't say anything. She looked at the money with her smart eyes, then looked around the stage. Her eyes swept across the curtain where Patrick was standing. He stepped back. He bumped into the Santa Claus. His hands quickly steadied Santa. Spying through the curtain, Patrick could see the older boy, the scout, was dumping his mission money in. "It looks like it will help a lot of hungry people." Then the younger boy poured in his money. He laughed like a pirate. They looked at Ebby. "C'mon," the older boy said, holding the lid for her. She was still looking around the stage. She dumped her money in and the older boy closed the lid. The boys started to march off. Ebby stood still. The older boy stopped and turned around.

"Aren't you coming?"

"In a minute."

"No way, you're not supposed to be up here alone."

"Yeah, you could steal all that money," the younger boy said.

"God is watching me," Ebby said, glancing toward the big crucifix.

The younger boy looked at the older boy to see if he would take such sass from a girl. The older boy bonked the younger boy on the ear. "Get moving!" They walked out the stage door into the hallway. Ebby stood still until the door closed. It was quiet.

Ebby was alone. She put her jar on the wood floor. It made a clunk. She stomped one foot and raised her left eyebrow with a smile. She stomped again and grinned. Clearing her throat, she addressed the sold-out crowd:

"Good evening ladies and gentlemen … Tonight at the Muny Opera, we have a really special girl who has been a sensation in London and Paris. Please welcome Ebby Hamilton!"

She took a bow then started dancing. Her feet soft-shoed left and right, all the way across the stage, then she twirled around into a few Nutcracker leaps. Patrick watched her waltz around the mission box with all the steps she had learned at the Monday Club without him. She held out her no-good-for-sports stick arms to receive a dance partner. It was just like he had pictured her dancing with him on the fairway. The feeling of the new thing flushed through his veins. He realized this was it.

Just like Jimmy had told him to get going with a girl, the way Jimmy had danced with Cindy at the Halloween party, this was his chance. All he had to do was step from behind the curtain and take her hands. Of course, she would be a little surprised. But then she would smile and they would move together to the music. She would look at him and understand everything. She would see it in his eyes—the new thing. Then who knows? Maybe go together to the mission carnival. Maybe the school picnic. Maybe get married. He took a deep breath and opened the curtain.

His shoe emerged from under the curtain like the leading tip of an invasion. A hand fell on his shoulder. He jumped and turned to face—Santa. He stepped back behind the curtain to prop Santa back up, but his tie got entangled in Santa's balsa wood grip. As he struggled to get free. Ebby sang to herself and danced alone.

La, la, la, la, la, la-la-, la, la, la, la…."

Her singing was like the music from a merry-go-round after it's too late to get on. Patrick started choking Santa. His cotton beard fell off. Santa was an old department store dummy, but he just wouldn't let go. Patrick shuffled with Santa, but it wasn't the same as dancing with Ebby. Then she stopped singing. He dragged Santa to the curtain and peeked through the slit. She was bending over to pick up her jar. She took it and started to walk off the stage.

He opened his lips to breathe out her name.

But before he could speak, she stopped. She stopped solid the way the gang used to when they heard a freight train coming. She hurried over to the mission box, opened the lid and grabbed a bunch of paper money. She wadded up the dough and stuck it in her skirt pocket, and danced off the stage singing.

"La, la, la, la, la, la-la, la, la, la...."

- chapter twenty-nine -

DEAD LEAVES BLEW ACROSS the blacktop playground as Patrick's class ran out to recess. In the sky, patchy clouds streaked across the sun, making the playground bright, then dark, then bright again. It was too cold for kickball. Patrick ran along the fence line dragging his fingertips across the chain link. The run felt good, because of the secret. He had not told anyone what he had seen Ebby do. And keeping such a big secret made his legs go. He ran until the cold air stung in his throat. Then he spotted Ebby. She was over by the girls. He started to walk toward her. Jimmy Purvis ran up to him.

"Patrick, God, what the hell happened? I heard somebody threw up on Cindy. Did you see it?"

He kept walking, watching the girls jump rope. "Oh, yeah, Cindy ... they sent her home to change."

Jimmy folded his arms together to keep warm, not having a coat. "Man, I can't believe it. You plan all your life for a date, then WHAM, vomit strikes. Were the chunks big?"

Patrick and Jimmy approached the girls. Jimmy kept talking. But Patrick did not hear him. He was looking at Ebby. She was standing with her back to him, playing with a pair of red clackers. The clackers, two hard plastic balls on a rope, flew up and down slamming into each other. They made a rapid *clack, clack, clack, clack* sound that cut through the air like gun shots. Jimmy pulled on Patrick's tie to get his attention.

"Hey, I *said*, do you think she'll still be able to go with me to the carnival?"

"Probably."

"God, for a Winston…."

Patrick watched Ebby skip into a jump rope hot box. She jumped faster and faster as the ropes blurred around her and all the girls chanted:

"Miss Mary Mack, Mack, Mack. All dressed in black, black, black. With silver buttons, buttons, buttons. All down her back, back, back…."

Ebby busted up laughing as the ropes caught her. She flipped her hair back and gathered it in a hair band. Jimmy saw Patrick staring at her.

"Hey, are you going to ask Ebby? We could go together. Maybe get your dad to drive us in his car. It has a good heater, right?"

Patrick nodded.

"OK, here's what you do. It's like sales. First, you got to sell yourself. Maybe say a few words about hockey. Then just ask her."

"OK."

Jimmy broke into a coughing fit from the combination of never wearing a coat and Winstons. He pushed Patrick toward Ebby and watched. Patrick walked toward her. He didn't really want to ask her to the mission carnival. Mostly he wanted to look in her eyes to tell her without words that he knew she stole the mission money. He would hold his eyes the way Mom's eyes looked when she ironed to Big Band Radio. He needed to let her know he still felt the new thing for her, no matter what. She was ten feet away. He walked toward her as another girl started to jump rope. The chanting got louder as he approached:

"Miss Lucy had a steamboat. The steamboat had a bell. Miss Lucy went to heaven. The steamboat went to hell … lo operator, give me number nine…."

He straightened his hair. He ran his eyes down Ebby's arm to her fingertips hanging at her side. He reached slowly to touch them. A loud yell came from the other end of the playground.

"SPIT PIT!"

Heads turned. Balls dropped. Ebby and everyone on the playground started to run. Patrick stood still watching the massive migration. Balls rolled. Kids ran past him. Ebby weaved into the crowd to get a choice spot along the spit pit railing. He jogged after her.

The spit pit was an ancient playground tradition dating back to the founding of the parish in the 1940s. No one knew how it started. But everyone understood the custom and respected it. The spit pit was a forty-foot deep stairwell leading to the basement of the priest's house. Whenever a ball, coat or hat landed in the pit, the owner would rush down the steps to retrieve it under a hail of spitting students. It was a ritual passed down from generation to generation without any written instructions.

Patrick reached the railing. The crowd blocked his view. Someone had thrown Sara Jibbs' mittens down there. Sarah was a kind, quiet girl who always did her homework. Mothers' Club playground guards shouted "Stop this at once. Stop this!" But it had no effect. Everyone chanted, "SPIT PIT, SPIT PIT, SPIT PIT...." Yellow leaves blew in the wind as Sara Jibbs took a deep breath and ran down the steps beneath the harking sounds of dozens of young throats.

Saliva enriched with lunch debris twirled toward the pit. Patrick saw Ebby spitting away and laughing. She leaned eagerly over the railing, full of life, without a trace of guilt from the robbery. A shot plastered Sara on the ear. The crowd cheered.

"Hey, you birds, get away from here!" yelled Father Maligan, leaning from a bathroom window with shaving cream on his face. "Go play by the nun's house!" He slammed the window shut. The crowd ran away from the railing laughing. Patrick positioned himself to intercept Ebby. He rehearsed his eyebrow movements—a caring Big Band Radio look. She was walking toward him.

Monsignor O'Day stepped out of the priest's house in his long black cassock. He flashed a yellow pack of Juicy Fruit. The whole playground ran over to him. "Monsignor, Monsignor, Monsignor...." Ebby ran past Patrick. He followed her. Jimmy Purvis ran up with a kick ball. The crowd was five students thick, everyone trying to touch him.

"All right now, here's the bet. A dollar says you can't kick that ball over the fence," Monsignor said.

The crowd parted. Jimmy stood by the dumpster. He kicked the ball. It pulled into the air toward the fence 200 feet away, but it fell short.

"Say, you owe me a buck," Monsignor said, "Anybody else?"

With no intention of paying, Jimmy melted into the crowd. Somebody threw the ball in from the outfield and a girl kicked it. She missed, too. Ebby got in line.

"Boy, I'm two dollars ahead," Monsignor said.

Three more boys tried, but they all landed short.

"Well, you kids owe me five bucks. When do I get my money?"

The kids laughed and Monsignor walked toward the school. His face changed to a look of official business. Ebby took the ball. She dropkicked it. It rose about 100 feet, then fell near the fence and bounced over. Everyone cheered.

"Hey, Monsignor! Look! It went over!" Patrick yelled.

Monsignor turned around. He squinted in the direction of the fence. The ball was bouncing by a backyard birdbath. He reached in his pocket and pulled out a fresh dollar bill. Ebby grabbed it.

"Thanks, Monsignor."

"I always pay my debts."

She skipped off with her dollar as Patrick watched her from the dumpster.

Monsignor put his hands in his cassock pockets and whistled an Irish song his mother used to sing. She was long dead. But Monsignor still thought of her. He climbed the side steps to the school under the statue of Mary Queen of Our Hearts on the church roof. Sister Mathilda with cataracts opened the side school door and bumped into him. She could vaguely see his black cassock and the red buttons. She acted sharp.

"Of course, Monsignor," she said.

"Sister Mathilda, how's that Cutlass?"

"Oh, it's a fine looking car."

"Well, if you ever get tired of it—"

"I know, you'd like to raffle it off again."

He pulled out his deck of cards and thumbed it. "Fundraising is an art."

"Like teaching," Sister Mathilda said, "Done best by those with experience."

He studied her eyes to see if he could make out the cataracts the principal had warned him about. He could only see that her eyes were bright blue, like the eyes of a girl who had wanted to be a nun someday, and had done so. "Yes, well, I've got to go. I'm going to help count the mission money. I hope there's more paper money than pennies." He half-bowed and went inside. Sister Mathilda raised her right hand and shook the bell as hard as she could, like she used to when she was a young nun. Patrick's class marched inside.

- chapter thirty -

THE AFTERNOON DRAGGED ON. First there was times tables. Everybody was supposed to be up to nine times nine. It was all memorization. And it was hard. Except for some people. The Roofus twins had rocketed to the outer boundaries of the universe—twelve times twelve. So Sister Mathilda stopped calling on them. Then there was a spelling bee. A girl named Ann with blonde hair was the champion today. She knew there was a hidden "a" in the word "orange." Then there was reading time. You could read any book you wanted to from the bookcase in the cloakroom. Most of the books smelled like the 1940s.

Patrick chose a book with pictures of a village where boys went barefoot and sheep ran in the street. He gazed at one picture a long time, hoping to transport himself there by concentration. But it never worked. He looked up and saw the two empty desks from the morning vomit incident. Sister Mathilda was at her desk correcting papers. The radiators by the windows were still hissing. The gold statue of Mary on the roof was watching.

Patrick never really thought about Mary anymore. He figured she was up there somewhere with Jesus and God the Father and everybody important, but they were all involved in high level projects, and he was just a kid. Once he had tried to get Mary's attention on a fishing trip. It was after a girl next to him caught a big catfish from a stocked pond. When Patrick asked her how she did it, she said she just kept saying Hail Marys until she got a bite. So, he tried it, secretly. He said about ten Hail Marys under his breath and watched his bobber. It was a really hot day and the sun was cooking his scalp through his hair. The bobber sat there motionless in the green water. He was sweating and the spit was drying up in his mouth from reciting Hail Marys. So, he reeled in and decided to go fish down the hill in the shade by the big lake with the adults. They had a cooler with sodas and snacks and laughter. He never caught anything that day.

Around two-thirty, Sister Mathilda stood up. She dipped a sponge in the water bucket and started to wipe down the chalkboard.

"Boys and girls, the time has come. School is over at three. In a few minutes it will be time to walk over to church and make your first confession. I know that you all will do a good job. You all know right from wrong." She squeezed the dirty chalk water into the bucket and dipped the sponge again. Her old hands pulled the sponge across an incorrect math problem. "It's a clean feeling to come out of confession. It's an even better feeling to receive your First Holy Communion. You'll do that on Saturday with your families watching. But today, first let's walk quietly to the bathroom so you can sit still during confession. Remember this is a solemn time. Prepare your hearts. Think about all you've done to fall short."

In the boys bathroom, bursts of suppressed laughter echoed off the tile walls as a line of boys pushed to run under an arch of urine streaming from a fat boy to the urinal four feet away. The fat boy counted quickly as each soul ran under his flow line. The school record for running under a urine arch was eighty-one times. Patrick had run under six times already. He circled around the fat boy and got in line again. The line moved quickly. The fat boy counted out loud.

"Seventy-five, seventy-six, seventy-seven...."

Patrick's turn was coming. Inside the fat boy, bladder pressure was suddenly diminishing. The arch of urine, which had maintained such steady curvature and lift, began to fluctuate.

"Seventy-eight, seventy-nine...."

Patrick ran under. He felt a hot shot across his back.

"Sorry, Patrick, you didn't make it," the fat boy said.

"We're never going to reach a perfect 100. It's just not humanly possible," another said.

The fat boy zipped up. "I tried. I held it all day."

Outside the bathroom, the boys and girls merged on the steps. They climbed toward the exit that led to church. There were kids from Patrick's and Ebby's second-grade classes. Patrick didn't want Ebby to find out about his wet shirt.

He broke out of the line and ran another flight of steps toward his classroom. He needed to change. Sister Mathilda was standing by the chalkboard. All the desks were empty. She looked at him.

"Is it Patrick?"

"Yes, sister."

"What are you doing here? Why aren't you with the others?"

"I need to change."

She came closer. She was so close, he could count her wrinkles and see her turkey neck move when she talked. "What's the matter?"

"Well, Sister, it's my Cub Scout uniform. Field trip at three."

She studied his eyes to see if he was hiding something. Behind his back, Patrick pulled at his shirt to peel the wet cotton off his skin. It was an awful feeling having somebody else's pee touching you.

"Patrick, you must feel pretty good right now."

"Sister?"

"I mean making your first confession. I mean finally being able to wipe the slate clean after *you know what*."

"What?"

"Ben Franklin!"

He looked to the side at all the empty desks.

She put her bony, bell-ringing hand on his shoulder. "You've had that on your soul for several months now, and today you can wipe it clean." Her arm made a sweep that took in the empty desks and some future graveyard waiting for them all. "Stealing like that! That was a mortal sin. You know what would have happened if you had died *before* you went to confession?" The radiator banged. She turned to lay the sponge on the chalk ledge. Patrick reached his hand behind his back to flap fresh air up his shirt. She brushed her hands together to shoo off the chalk dust. "Well, you better change. But do me a favor?"

"Yes, Sister?"

"Throw out my dirty water, will you?"

Patrick took her water to the window and opened it. He could see the second graders from both classes filing into the church. He saw Ebby standing in line. He threw out the dirty water. It splashed on the dead grass below two floors below. He closed the window and hurried to the cloakroom to get his Cub Scout uniform.

- chapter thirty-one -

MOM HAD IRONED HIS CUB SCOUT uniform until the creases in the blue shirt and pants were extra sharp. The Cub Scouts stood for something. With Big Band Radio playing, she had leaned into the iron with extra feeling. Nearby, Patrick had practiced the oath, to be honest, courteous, thoughtful, kind, obedient, prompt, and Mom had opened her sewing drawer to let him have a special gift—her father's Boy Scout knife. Her late father, Patrick Senior, had risen to the rank of Eagle Scout, and later received a battlefield commission for bravery under fire in the Argonne Forest in World War One. And he had told Mom to marry a Catholic man and raise a Catholic family. Admittedly, the family had fallen off a cliff with the Ben Franklin incident, but now there was change. Patrick and John had stayed out of trouble for almost three months. They were climbing back uphill. And Patrick was about to make his first confession and communion. The new baby was coming soon—maybe before Christmas. Wouldn't that be something? The family could all arrive just a little late for Monsignor O'Day's big Mass. Everyone in the parish would see Mom going up the aisle holding the pink dressed newborn. Monsignor might make some remark the way only he could. "Oh, I see another tax deduction." And then at communion, Patrick would go up for a host with John and Mom and Dad.

Patrick ran out of school in his Cub Scout uniform. The blacktop between the school and the church was empty. He ran across it, opened the outer church door and put his bag with the urine-stained shirt by the heater that was always blowing. He straightened his yellow and blue-striped neckerchief and opened the inner door.

Inside, the janitor was buffing the floors with an electric waxer. It was as loud as a tornado drill. The girls were seated on one side and the boys on the other. Everybody was waiting around in the dark with nothing to see by but the cloudy, stained-glass daylight and purgatory candles. Patrick made the sign of the cross and knelt in the back of the boys' section. He started to say an Our Father, but got watching the swirling cotton heads of the floor buffer and lost track. The janitor was trying to get the place perfect for the first communion celebration. Patrick made the sign of the cross and sat down. He looked around for Ebby. She was across the aisle in the back pew of the girls' section looking right at him. She noticed his uniform and smiled. She saluted him. He felt the new thing.

Monsignor O'Day and Father Maligan burst out of the door behind the altar. Everyone looked at them. They were in charge. They wore long black cassocks. Monsignor O'Day waved to the boys and girls, while Father Maligan, his brain throbbing from the floor buffer, fired a glance at the janitor. The janitor flipped off the buffer. Its engines whirled down. He retreated backwards toward the storage closet. Monsignor O'Day held up his hand to get everyone's attention.

"OK, kids, we're ready to hear your confessions. We're running a little late, due to some trouble counting the mission money. So I want you all to have your sins ready to rattle off as soon as you hit the kneeler. We don't want anybody to miss the bus. Half of you go to Father Maligan, and half to me. And God bless you." He made a quick blessing gesture in the air and hurried over to his confessional.

This was it. The students in the front row got up to go tell their sins. Everyone was quiet. No more running under urine. In just a couple of minutes they would all have to go into that little room—alone. They would have to close the door behind them and kneel on the kneeler. Under their knees they would feel the padded kneeler click down an eighth of an inch, activating the electric, "no vacancy" cross light outside above the confessional door. Then it would be too late. Then there would be no more time to rehearse lines. The only thing to do would be to stare forward and wait for the trap window to slide open like waiting for the floor to drop out at your hanging.

Patrick watched as the front row of boys filed past him. Some went left. Some went right. Jimmy Purvis passed, flashing a sly grin, and holding his palm open in front of Patrick's face. Patrick saw a paragraph of miniature writing on Jimmy's hand. Jimmy had scribbled the Act of Contrition and other notes. Patrick thought about his own sins: Being on the tracks, lying, saying SHIT, smoking, robbing the Ben Franklin … Maybe Sister Mathilda was right. Get a clean slate. He looked over at Ebby. She was sitting in the back of the girls' pews swinging one leg back and forth. She sneaked a piece of gum in her mouth.

A muffled disturbance could be heard from Father Maligan's confessional. Maligan, who was hard of hearing, was asking children to "speak up, speak up." His nasally, aggravated brogue buzzed around the church marble. Everyone listened. From the center pews children could hear the victim—a high-pitched girl—confessing her sins. She had been impatient with her sister and yelled at her. "Not so loud, you bird, I've got a headache," Maligan yelled. Hearing this, a group of students in line for Father Maligan retreated toward Monsignor O'Day's confessional. A door opened. Jimmy Purvis came out. He had just confessed his sins to Monsignor O'Day. Everyone looked to see if he was changed. He looked worse. Jimmy whispered some new development to the boys in line for Monsignor O'Day. They all switched sides again back to Father Maligan.

Jimmy made his way to Patrick and leaned over to him. "If you stole anything, don't go to O'Day."

"Why not?"

"He says a thief can't be forgiven, unless he returns what he stole first. I never heard that shit, did you? I've got to go warn the others. Can you think of any others who stole?"

Patrick looked over at Ebby. "No."

"I guess I'm going to have to buy my dad about a carton of Winstons. Damn, I can't afford that with the carnival and Cindy."

A veiny, white hand soaring from a black sleeve grabbed Jimmy's ear. It was Sister Mathilda. She had slipped in from behind without a sound. "Young man, get over to your own class and get to work praying. This isn't carnival!" Jimmy hurried to his pew and knelt like he was on death row, rubbing his ear.

Sister Mathilda genuflected and knelt in the pew behind Patrick. She heaved a sigh. Patrick wished she had knelt behind somebody else. He stole a glance at Ebby. Ebby was pushing her tongue through some gum almost blowing a bubble. Ebby looked back at the clock. Patrick looked, too. It was seven minutes before three o'clock. Ebby stood up. It wasn't her turn. But she got up and walked toward Monsignor O'Day's confessional. No one had warned her. Patrick stood up.

"Sit down, Patrick, are you better than the others?" Can't you wait your turn?" Sister Mathilda said.

"Yes, sister." He sat back down. Sister Mathilda was still kneeling behind him. He twisted his Cub Scout neckerchief. He looked over at Ebby. She was in line for confession with two kids ahead of her.

"What are you looking for over there? Have you got a girlfriend? Is that it? Are you here to get married, or go to confession? *Patrick ... the time.* This is All Souls Day. Say a prayer for some soul in purgatory. Surely you must know some dead people."

"No, sister."

"What about your grandmother?"

He had forgotten all about Nana. He was ashamed and knelt to pray. He tried to remember her. But after Nana died, her face had gotten blurry. He remembered how she had told him to be good and was going to help him go to the Monday Club with Ebby when he saw her in the grocery store. She had always been good. She was always friendly and doing things to show her love.

The door in front of Ebby opened. Patrick stole a glance, then bowed his head like he was praying. He needed to warn Ebby somehow. Unfortunately, the student who just went in was one of the Roofus twins. He would not have enough sins to fill the time. Ebby had only one student standing between her and Monsignor O'Day. O'Day would surely ask her if she had returned the stolen mission money. Patrick looked at the clock. It was five minutes to three.

"Can I get in line now, Sister? I have to leave at three for the field trip."

"The field trip? Everyone's in such a big hurry to rush out into the world. Where is this field trip?"

Patrick started to get up. "I forgot."

"*You forgot?* That reminds me," she said grasping his sleeve, "did you say a prayer yet for the *most forgotten soul* in purgatory?"

"Who?"

She let go of his sleeve. Maybe her retirement was near. No one listened to her advice anymore. She had lectured about the most forgotten soul and how he needed help from the living. It was what All Souls Day was all about. But Patrick, and probably everyone else, had forgotten about him. Her blue cataract eyes moistened. Patrick sat down.

"Sister?"

She reached up her sleeve and pulled out a handkerchief. Patrick watched her unfold it. It was raggedy and thinned out. She dabbed her eyes. Patrick watched her. Her turkey chin vibrated. "I'm sorry. I don't mean to keep you from your field trip. It's important, too. It's just that someday, Patrick…." She looked around at the saint statues and the flickering purgatory candles. "I know someday some new teacher will have my class. And me, I'll be, who knows where." She shrugged and blew her nose. "I haven't got any family or anyone living who really thinks about me." Patrick covered his mouth and nose with his neckerchief to protect himself from her afternoon nun breath. "It's just that when All Souls Day comes, I wonder if maybe someday I'll end up… the most forgotten soul."

Patrick felt sorry for Sister Mathilda. He wanted to cheer her up. He searched his mind for something positive to say. Then he looked up at her. "Sister, you won't be forgotten. You've done something no other teacher has done."

"What?"

"You won the Cutlass."

She put her face in her hands. Patrick thought he'd better kneel back down a while. He stared at the wood grain on the pew in front of him and tried to say a prayer for the most forgotten soul. He could picture some old man down there, maybe a starved-looking guy with torn pants trying to carry rocks up a hill with flames licking at the path. He got halfway through a Hail Mary when he heard the confessional door open again. He looked over. Ebby was next. She was standing right next to the door. In less than a minute she would face Monsignor O'Day. Sister Mathilda coughed. Patrick tried again to concentrate on the most forgotten soul. He started another Hail Mary, because the first one had unraveled. He wanted to get back to the old man with torn pants. But this time all he could think about was Ebby. He saw her stealing the money. What if something should happen to her? He imagined her trying to carry big rocks with her skinny arms. The confessional door opened. Ebby started to go in.

The church clock chimed the three o'clock hour.

Monsignor O'Day opened the center door. He stepped out. He waved to the kids. "That's enough for today. We'll get the rest of you tomorrow. Don't anyone miss your ride." He waved goodbye to the students. Father Maligan came out too, winding his watch, holding it to his ear. Ebby skipped along the back wall toward the exit. Patrick started to get up. But Sister Mathilda looked at him.

"Patrick, thank you."

"No problem, catch you tomorrow."

"No wait...."

He sat back down. She leaned back in her pew. She rubbed the stiffness in her bell-ringing hand. "It's just that with teaching, a nun wonders if her students are paying attention." He looked over her shoulder for Ebby. Sister Mathilda organized the hymnals in a neat stack. "Time gets us all. All of you are growing up. Someday you'll drive downtown to work. I won't be around." He realized she was still talking to him. He looked at her. "Try to remember one thing." He could see the students piling out of the door escaping into the light. "It's all about love, Patrick. I know you don't really understand love at your age." Ebby yelled "hooray" in the doorway. "But if you love, you *do*." Sister Mathilda made a gesture that took in the altar and the saint statues and church history. "And if you love someone here on earth, you can only show it by what you do. You understand?"

He nodded. He did understand—sort of—but really, he just hoped Sister Mathilda wasn't going to want to hug him after their heart-to-heart talk.

She gave him a nod like he could go. He jumped up and ran out the door in his Cub Scout uniform, grabbing the bag with his pee-soaked clothes on the way.

- chapter thirty-two -

EBBY SHUT THE DOOR to her family's Cadillac and it flew away without any chance for Patrick to warn her. He watched her car go down Main Street and thought about her soul. Then he turned around and spit and walked back toward the school to go on the field trip.

The Cub Scout troop of nine boys always met by the flagpole. He walked to the flagpole and nodded hello to the boys. They said hi back, but without much fizz. Their parents had warned them about Patrick. Every parent in the parish knew about the Ben Franklin incident. And so did every boy in the Cub Scout troop. They were gentle boys who had never stolen anything. They had never ridden on a boxcar—never even been on the tracks before. They were boys whose hearts were still in the original box, unopened. They had never talked to a girl. They never felt the new thing. They were the sons of parish leaders—ushers, collection-plate passers, men who used power tools on their son's pinewood derby cars and won. They were boys who thought life was collecting Lincoln pennies, or going door to door to sell light bulb "home packs" to raise money for the troop. Patrick studied them from a distance.

One was a tall, skinny boy with big ears. Another was a bucktooth kid with something like Crisco in his hair. Another boy protected himself from thought by constantly humming the theme song to the TV show *Flipper*. There was also a boy who was plagued by the nagging problem of having his pants catch in his butt crack all day long. He was constantly reaching around to pull his pants free. Alone, they were boys on the outskirts of acceptance. But together, on Wednesday only, they met at the flag pole as a troop unified by blue and yellow fabric. Patrick kicked the flagpole and surrendered himself to their company.

The school bus pulled away. Liberated children ran home for reruns and Twinkies while the troop waited for their den mother. Mrs. Dillsworth finally pulled up in a rusty station wagon. Everyone crowded in. She passed out carrot sticks. They were dry. She asked everyone what they learned in school. Long division, said the boy with big ears. Patrick wanted to roll down his window to throw out his carrot stick, but the window was busted out and duct-taped with clear plastic Saran Wrap. The car pulled away from the school. Mrs. Dillsworth led the boys in a round of singing one of the modern guitar church songs, something about rain drops and windows and joy. She sang in an opera voice, as her station wagon struggled down Main Street coughing out smoke.

+ + + +

The smoldering troop wagon parked in the lot above the Webster hobby shop. The boys ran down the spiral staircase to the street. Traffic streamed by and people drifted in and out of shops. The boys stopped by the hobby shop window to look at a new monster model kit for sale. It was another Aurora plastic model, the same company that had made the Wolfman. The new model showed a skeleton in raggedy clothes chained to a dungeon wall. His jaw was open like he had been dead for years. There was an extra skull on the floor next to him and some plastic rats sucking marrow. The window banner read:

HEY KIDS, WE HAVE THE LATEST MONSTER MODEL:
"THE FORGOTTEN PRISONER"

Mrs. Dillsworth looked over the boys' shoulders. "Who would design such a toy? C'mon boys, let's not be late for our field trip."

Patrick brought up the rear as they crossed the street by the Ben Franklin and the Rexall. He visualized the boys and Mrs. Dillsworth crossing the street as skeletons. A car drove by with a dead man behind the wheel. The flesh on his cheeks had holes in it. Rats ran out of the sewer toward Mrs. Dillsworth's anklebone. Somebody shouted, "Let's go in Ben Franklin for candy." Mrs. Dillsworth said OK. Patrick waited outside. He thought about the Ben Franklin man with the sad eyes and then about Ebby and the music of her dancing on the stage earlier in the day. *"La, la, la, la, la-la, la, la, la, la...."* Why did she steal the money? Didn't she want to go to heaven? He stood there looking down a sidewalk grate at foil gum wrappers. A Bi-State bus fumed by. A man in a trench coat and hat came out of the Rexall, sneezing. He pulled out a handkerchief and a twenty-dollar bill fell on the sidewalk. It blew over by Patrick, and his eyes got big.

Maybe God meant for him to take it, so he could pay back what Ebby stole so she could be forgiven. The man stood there hacking up phlegm. Patrick picked up the twenty. But it didn't feel right. Maybe it was a temptation to see if Patrick would steal again. The man blew his nose. Patrick realized God wanted him to tell the man he dropped it, so the man would give Patrick the twenty as a reward. Then he could pay off Ebby's sin.

Patrick spoke up. *"Sir,"* he said holding out the twenty.

"What? Did I drop that? Hey, you're a good'n honest man. Thanks, here's a nickel."

The other boys came out of Ben Franklin chewing Sugar Daddies and Bazooka Joe and treasures of chocolate. Patrick brought up the rear as they crossed the street into the bank. An intense dislike for scouting rose in his throat. He felt trapped with a losing troop on a boring field trip. Nothing exciting could happen in a bank.

The lobby smelled of burnt coffee and stale perfume. The air was a little warmer than the Straub's frozen food section, but still cool to save money on the heating bill. Secretaries with bulletproof hair piles typed forms. Men in white, long-sleeved shirts and careful ties worked the teller's cages. Patrick looked around. There was a Lion's Club gumball machine. A decal on the curved glass said: "DO SOMETHING FOR OTHERS."

Patrick put in the nickel. He cranked it. The nickel stuck. No gum would come out. He was shaking the gumball machine when the elevator opened. A glowing man in a white suit and silver toupee stepped off.

"God bless America … the troops are here," he said.

"Are you Mr. Karpfinger?" asked Mrs. Dillsworth.

"Call me Fred." He buttoned his jacket. He was an older man with thick eyeglasses and a twenty-dollar gold piece tie pin. He whacked an official envelope in his hand.

Mrs. Dillsworth nodded to him, "We're here for the tour. How are you today?"

"I'm great, just great. I feel better than an eight-hundred dollar runaway slave." He smiled with positive-thinking vitality and patted the heads of a few boys nearby. "Boys, I want you to know first off, that I was once a scout myself. Scouting is one of the most positive things in life. It teaches you independence." He flagged down a passing secretary. "Marsha, hon', could you please get me a cup of coffee? I'm on a tour."

"Yes, Mr. Karpfinger."

He remembered Mrs. Dillsworth and asked if she wanted a cup. But she said coffee was bad for her choir voice. The boys followed Karpfinger through the lobby as he lectured on the bank, gesturing around with his official envelope. His reedy voice echoed off the green marble as the tour progressed. "Men, this is our state-of-the-art lobby. The floors and walls are made of marble, same kind you find in your finer churches. And up above the window there, you see our lovely mural of downtown in the good old days."

The boys looked. The painting showed a steamboat stopping on the St. Louis riverfront. Smoke drifted out the stacks. Women in puff-sleeved dresses with corseted figures watched from the high ground. Businessmen eager for their cargo looked at pocket watches. Horses hitched to pull supply wagons stood in the heat ready to pull. A row of black men carried sacks and barrels on their backs up the levee to the wagons.

"Yes, those were the days. Now, over here let's walk quietly through our loan department." The boys followed him past a set of desks with bankers listening to loan applicants. A blonde housewife was smiling as her husband signed the final papers on a home loan. "We've made it," she said. The boys walked past another table where a black man in a suit and tie was watching a banker read over his application for a loan.

"Collateral is everything," the loan officer said.

"I'm working just as hard as everybody else," the black man said.

The boys followed Karpfinger along the row of teller's windows. Customers were in line. Some made deposits, some withdrawals. Money flowed. A man with a red nose counted a fat stack of money. He saw Patrick staring at the loot.

"What are you going to do with all that?" Patrick said.

"Gamble it," he said winking at the teller. The teller smiled.

Patrick brought up the rear as the tour marched down a back hallway into the safety deposit room. The boys stopped. Above them was a stained-glass skylight. Around them they could see the rich oak walls honeycombed with brass safety deposit boxes. There was an altar in the center for depositors to work on. Karpfinger cleared his throat and straightened his toupee. Patrick listened from the back row.

"Boys, some things in life are precious. That's what this room is for. You never know when your house might burn down. Houses are made of wood. But not this bank. It's all cold steel and marble." He slapped the marble table.

"If you ever want to hide something precious, this is the place. Are there any questions?"

A boy raised his hand.

"Yes, you there."

"What about all this wood in here? Won't it burn?"

Karpfinger clapped his hands and pointed at the boy. "*You, sir*, are paying attention. This wood, it's just ornamental. Behind it, the steel safety deposit boxes are able to withstand temperatures hotter than h-e-double-cue sticks." He banged on the deposit boxes to show their strength, and some heirloom china shifted inside one of them. "Yes, this is where you put things that are precious. Any more questions?"

Another boy raised his hand. It was the boy whose pants always clung to the crack in his butt. He pulled his pants free and asked, "What's precious?"

"Excellent question. Let me think now...." The secretary named Marsha walked in. She handed Karpfinger his coffee. He looked at her. He started to take a sip, but stopped to say, "Precious has to do with *feeling*." He looked at Marsha again and raised his eyebrows. He took a sip. His face puckered and he spit it back in the cup. "*Sheeesh*, Marsha, this is burnt. Let's make a fresh pot."

"Yes, sir."

"Another thing, could you deliver this envelope to the president's office?"

"Yes, sir."

He handed it to her. She took his cup, too. The boys followed him down a dark hallway to the vault room. He positioned his back so no one could spy on him. He spun the combination on the nickel-plated, five-inch-thick vault door. It clicked. He twirled a steel captain's wheel. He pulled the vault open. They stepped in. It was cooler inside, like Jesse James' hideout at Meramec Caverns. The air smelled like paper money. Patrick looked around. The paper money was out of reach. There was a table in the back with inch-thick stacks of cash. On the floor in the front of the vault were bags of pennies and a broken water cooler and cardboard promotional signs.

"Don't anybody touch anything," Mrs. Dillsworth said.

Karpfinger chuckled. "It's all right. All the paper money is locked up. Even I can't get to it. You need three keys." He nodded toward the thinly spaced steel bars separating the Cub Scouts from the paper money. "Now, kids, I want you all to look in front of me at this stack of pennies. Try to lift this sack while I say a few word about money ... the stuff of life."

Karpfinger bent over and struggled to pick up the fifty-pound sack. His gut hung over his belt. His toupee tilted. His glasses fell off. The pennies rose up six-inches off the ground. He dropped them on the floor. The bag went THUNK. Karpfinger straightened his toupee and tucked in his shirt. "Man, that's heavy. Go ahead boys see if you can lift it." Karpfinger put his glasses back on. Patrick tried first while Karpfinger spoke about money.

"Money has been around since the dawn of civilization. The oldest coin goes back to five hundred years before Christ. Now what does that tell us?"

Patrick pulled on the burlap bag and held his breath. But it was too heavy. He gave up. The boy with big ears raised his hand. "It tells us to save early, so the compound interest will make our money grow."

Karpfinger was amazed. "Super answer! Do you have an account here?"

"No, sir."

"Well, see me afterward. The point, though, is that money is the only thing that lasts." The boys took turns trying to lift the sack, each one grunting and yanking on the burlap neck. "Boys, look at the facts. We're all going to die. The pennies in this sack will outlast us. So the thing we need to do now is work to get as much money as we can and put it in the bank." Patrick's mind began to wander. He was watching the bag of pennies, thinking about Ebby. She had robbed the mission carnival and needed to pay it back to be forgiven. "Someday, boys, you'll all fall in love with some girl. You may want to marry her and raise a good Catholic family." He turned quickly to Mrs. Dillsworth and whispered. "*This is* the Catholic group, isn't it?"

"Yes, sir."

"That's right the Lutheran group is Thursday. We get so many." The Cub Scouts watched the sack of pennies. The boy who always hummed "Flipper" was humming as he tried to lift it. He stopped humming. It was too heavy. Patrick looked around the outer vault. He looked at the broken water cooler, the kind they would probably have in purgatory. He looked at the pretty girl on the cardboard advertising sign. Her skin was bleached from beckoning customers in the window all summer. The caption beneath her said: "IF YOU NEED A LOAN, WE UNDERSTAND."

Patrick looked at the sign, then at the banker talking. "Someday, boys you're gonna grow up, get married and work downtown," Karpfinger said. Patrick turned away from the back row and looked through the bars at the paper money. Karpfinger was wiping his glasses with his necktie while he lectured. "You'll work all day in a suit and tie for some son-of-a-gun boss and love it. Why? Because that's what it's all about. You'll know deep down you're doing good for the ones you love." Patrick touched the narrow bars. The metal was cold.

He thought about Ebby facing Monsignor O'Day in the confessional. He wondered if he could reach the paper money in the vault. He looked at the troop. They all had their backs turned to him. He looked at the pile of paper money. He shot a quick glance at Karpfinger and Mrs. Dillsworth. They were in front of the troop looking at the sack of pennies. All clear.

Patrick slipped his fingers through the thinly spaced bars. The bars were too tight for an adult to squeeze through. But Patrick fit. The bars smooshed his long sleeve Cub Scout uniform against his skin as he glided his arm in deeper. His fingers shadowed above a stack of twenties. Karpfinger continued.

"Love, family, community, that's what stacks up...."

But the nearest stack was beyond reach. Patrick tried to pull his arm out. It was stuck at the elbow. "You'll drive home to Webster each night knowing you're doing right by your family...." Patrick twisted and pulled until his arm came free. He got out his dead grandfather's Boy Scout pocketknife. He opened the blade and inserted his arm, blade first, through the bars. "And what will you be doing? You'll be making money ... money, money, money. That's nothing to be ashamed of ... it's something to be *proud* of." The leading edge of the blade slipped under the paper band holding together a stack of twenties. "Money is what allows us to *lift up* our feelings for the ones we love."

The stack of twenties lifted off the table, dangling from the tip of the blade. It flapped like a pelican as it made the journey toward the bars. It started to wobble. The boy with buckteeth and Crisco in his hair hoisted the bag of pennies an inch off the ground. He dropped the sack. THUD.

At that very instant, the stack of twenties slipped off the tip of the knife. But before it hit the floor, the cub scouts started clapping. No one heard the twenties hit the floor. Patrick looked around. Everyone had their backs to him, watching Karpfinger smile. Karpfinger gestured with his glasses in hand. "So, what will you do when you finally get your hands on some real money?"

Patrick crouched down and grabbed the stack of twenties. It came through the bars into his hands. "Hopefully, you'll think of others. What can you do for others? Sometimes people need a loan." Patrick unzipped his pants and put the stack between his pants and his underwear. "It's important, though, to never borrow more than you need." Patrick pulled the stack out of his pants, and removed a solitary twenty-dollar bill. He put the twenty in his side pocket for Ebby. He straightened the stack and wound up to toss it back on the table. But before he could throw it, Karpfinger called him.

"You back there…."

Patrick jammed the money into his pocket. Everyone turned around and looked at him. Karpfinger put on his glasses. "Come here, young man." Patrick walked through the troop to the front, closing the blade to his scout knife. He put the knife in his pocket with the cash.

"Yes, sir?"

"How much money have you got on you?"

"Sir?"

"Let's just pretend you needed a loan. Now, if the bank was to loan you whatever you needed for some emergency, really it's not the bank's money. It's money from your friends here, your fellow depositors. You would pay them back wouldn't you?"

"Yes, sir."

"You see, that's what's *so great* about money and banking. It allows your money that you deposit to do something good. Your money is doing for others, helping people with problems you could never imagine."

Mrs. Dillsworth cupped her hand to Patrick's ear and whispered. He pulled up his zipper just as the secretary walked in. She handed Karpfinger his coffee. He took a sip. It was good this time. "Marsha, you're precious." He gave her the googly eyes again, but she looked the other way.

"Thank you, sir, the bank president was asking after you."

"Oh, tell him I'll be right over. Boys, that concludes our tour today. I want you all to pick up a new account form. C'mon, now let's clear out of the vault. Got to lock 'er up."

Patrick looked back toward the bars. The stack of twenties felt big and conspicuous in his pocket. Mrs. Dillsworth put her guiding hand on Patrick's shoulder and directed him out the door. He stepped out with all the other boys. Karpfinger shut the vault. He spun the wheel. The boys walked into the main lobby. Patrick could feel the money pressing against his thigh as he walked. He didn't want to borrow more than he needed. He looked around to see if anyone was staring at him. The adult world was still functioning. A lady in a wool coat walked by to make a deposit. The troop walked up to the new accounts table. A man in a white shirt gave them each a brochure. Mrs. Dillsworth led them toward the front door. They walked out onto the street. The doors shut behind them. Patrick looked around. Cars were going by. It looked like a regular day. He stood still looking back at the bank while the troop started to cross the street.

"Mrs. Dillsworth?

"Yes, Patrick."

"I have to go to the bathroom."

"Can't you hold it?"

"No."

"Is it one or two?"

"Both!" Patrick ran back in the bank. He saw Karpfinger standing on the elevator adjusting his toupee for a visit with the bank president as the elevator doors closed. Patrick looked around. Secretaries were typing. Customers were coming and going. The new account representative was talking on the phone.

"Young man, may I help you?" a secretary said. It was Marsha.

"Can I use your bathroom?"

"I thought maybe you had to go. I saw your zipper open in the vault."

He went to the men's room. No one was in there. He looked in the mirror. He was breathing through his mouth panting on the glass. His neckerchief was crooked. He left it that way. He went in the stall. He closed the door behind him. He put the stack of twenties on top of the toilet tank. He unzipped his pants and urinated. The urine made suds rise in the water like a horseshoe. He wondered what to do. He wasn't sure. He zipped up. He got out the separate twenty—the one he was borrowing for Ebby, and put it in his Knucklehead Smith wallet. He didn't want to take more money than he needed, money that could do something good for someone else who needed it. So, he took a piece of toilet paper, the last piece dangling from the roll, and laid it on top of the twenties to hide it. Somebody would find it later and put it back in the vault. Some janitor. He flushed the toilet and left. He ran outside the bank so fast he knocked down a lady on the sidewalk carrying a sack of pennies. It was Mrs. Heimlich the heavy-set cafeteria lady making a deposit.

"Sorry," he said helping her up.

"I thought scouts were supposed to help people," she said. He apologized again and ran across the street. He flew up the spiral staircase and hopped in Mrs. Dillsworth's station wagon. Exhaust was pouring out.

"Everything come out OK?" Mrs. Dillsworth said. The troop all laughed at Patrick. They drove away.

Inside the bank, the black man who had just been rejected for a loan walked into the bathroom. He was mad that he'd worked so hard, and it hadn't made a lick of difference. Then he saw the money with the bank logo on the paper band. *What the...?* He wheezed with astonishment and picked it up. He smelled it. It was real all right. Stretching to his tiptoes, he peeked over the top of the stall left and right. All clear. With no one watching, the money went straight into his pocket—then he stopped. He was mad, but he wasn't a thief. He took it out and shook his head, thinking about what to do. Then, with a wild grin, he started flushing the money down the toilet one bill at a time. The toilet backed up. He tossed the rest of the bills in the water, dropped his pants, sat down.

"I'll give them collateral," he muttered.

After a few minutes, he got back up, tucked in his shirt, fastened his belt and straightened his tie. He looked down and saw a hot, brown, angry turd, floating on a sea of twenties, and laughed with a vengeance.

- chapter thirty-three -

THAT SAME AFTERNOON Ebby lay on her brass bed crying. Her father had just talked to her about it all. Now her mother was sitting on the bed trying to reassure her. She petted Ebby's hair.

"Ebby, it won't be so bad, you'll see. Tomorrow will be a new day. Tonight at the carnival you'll just have to tell them."

"It's so hard."

"I know, but sometimes we all have to change. You get ready and in a little while we'll drive you up there. We'll tell them as a family. OK?"

"OK. Does Raven know?"

"Yes, but I told him not to tease you about this or make it worse than it is."

Her mom left the room. Ebby wiped her eyes and got off the bed. She combed her hair in the mirror. She put down the brush and looked at the dollhouse on the table. She put her miniature family in their miniature beds, and carefully hinged the dollhouse shut. She locked the latch tight. She looked in the window at them. "Get a good night's sleep, tomorrow will be a new day."

++++

Jimmy Purvis's teeth chattered as he banged on the back door at Patrick's house. He was wearing a red Cardinals baseball cap, but no coat. Patrick's family was eating dinner. They were seated around the new and larger table. It was an office surplus table—an old boardroom table from dad's work with drawers on the side. They looked over and gave Jimmy the sign. He let himself in and immediately sat on the heater.

"Where's your coat, Jimmy?" Mom said.

"Oh, I'm warm-blooded. I don't need one," Jimmy said rubbing his hands. "Hey, you got a new table."

Dad wiped his mouth with a napkin. "Yes, Jimmy, the family is expanding. This is a boardroom table from my work. A lot of big decisions have been made around this table. Eat your string beans, Teddy."

"So you boys are going to the mission carnival tonight?" Mom said.

"Yeah, I guess Patrick told you. I got a date."

"What?" Dad said, putting down his fork. "I didn't have a date until high school."

Jimmy stood up and looked at himself in the mirror and wiped his runny nose. "Well, it's not a *real* date with a car, but me and Cindy ... she's in Patrick's class ... me and her are going to the booths together." Jimmy took off his ball cap and looked at his hair from all sides in the mirror.

"Hey, that's great," Mom said scratching her pregnant belly, "I think that's wonderful."

"What grade are you in?" Dad said.

"Same as Patrick."

"I know, but what's that, again?" Dad said.

"Second," Patrick said.

"I don't know what those nuns are teaching you boys," Dad said.

Mom felt the baby kick and looked at her three sons. They were sitting there dateless.

"Well, they have to start sometime. Boys liking girls ... girls liking boys ... It could happen in our family."

Patrick drank his milk. John watched *Lost in Space*. Dad cut his carrots in short, tense chops. Teddy opened a drawer on the new boardroom table slowly. He looked to see if Mom and Dad were watching. They weren't. With a deft motion, he edged his string beans over the side of his plate, plopped them into the drawer and slid it shut.

++++

The boys climbed out of the Falcon in front of the school. It was dark and chilly. Except for Jimmy, they zipped up their coats. They could see their breath in the floodlights that shined from behind the Vatican bushes onto the school and church. The illuminated gold state of Mary Queen of Our Hearts still stood watch on the church roof. The Roofus twins rode by on a bicycle built for two with a math club sticker on the front basket. Dad honked his horn and yelled out the window.

"Hey, Patrick, come here a minute … by yourself."

Patrick looked at Jimmy, then walked over to the car window. Dad cleared his throat and told him softly, "Listen, Patrick, don't let all this talk about having a date bother you. Your mother may push that, but that's just because her father was always playing love songs on the piano, and he gave his girls so much attention after their mother died. In the real world, it's not like that. It's getting to work early and doing your work right that counts. Understand?"

Patrick wasn't sure what to think. "OK."

Dad called over to the others, "Boys, I want you all to stick together and stay out of trouble. I'll be back to pick you up later. I'd go, but there's an important program tonight on the Lincoln conspiracy."

They waved to him. He drove off.

"I guess we should split up here and meet later," Jimmy said.

Patrick and Jimmy ran ahead. John held hands with his little brother Teddy. "Why are we going alone?" Teddy asked. As a kindergartner, Teddy did not yet know about nighttime school functions. He had never been to the school after dark. He did not yet know how the darkness and absence of uniforms destroyed the authority structure that ruled by day. At night, no one stuck together. At night, feelings long held inside could be let out. Someone might throw a partially-chewed caramel from across the room into a nun's hair. Someone might even hold a girl's hand. The unstructured freedom of a night event made anything possible. Patrick and Jimmy climbed the steps toward the gym wondering what the night would bring.

- chapter thirty-four -

"JUST DON'T CROWD US," Jimmy said to Patrick. "Me and Cindy, we got a way about us. We might want to go to the booths alone after a while." He flashed a fist full of dollar bills at Patrick.

"Wow, that's a lot. I thought that for confession you needed to buy back the Winstons you stole," Patrick said.

"Don't remind me," Jimmy said, getting anxious. "I'll have to make up something in confession. It's just that with me and Cindy … it's like … well, if you ever get that feeling for a girl, you'll understand."

An eighth-grade Boy Scout took their quarter admission and ink stamped the back of their hands with a heart. They walked in the gym. It was bright inside. Hundreds of loud, laughing kids were crowding the aisles browsing from booth to booth. Patrick and Jimmy walked up to the ticket table.

"Get your tickets. Buy as many as you can. It's for a good cause," the Boy Scout said.

Jimmy elbowed Patrick. "Keep your eyes peeled for her." Jimmy laid down three bucks. The eighth-grade Boy Scout tore off a foot long roll of bright red tickets. Jimmy grabbed them.

"How about you, kid?" the Boy Scout said. Patrick reached in his pocket for some quarters, being careful not to pull out the envelope with the twenty-dollar bill from the bank. He offered four quarters for the cause.

"Hey, last of the big spenders," Jimmy said.

The Boy Scout gave Patrick some tickets. They walked along up the first aisle of booths. There was a math booth for kids with intelligence. There was a booth with yellow rubber ducks floating in some water. You were supposed to guess one with the right number on the bottom. There was a Lollipop ball booth. It featured a Styrofoam ball stuck with Lollipops. You were supposed to choose one and if the bottom of the stick was colored, you won a Ben Franklin gift certificate. There was a tabletop hockey booth where you could win an orange driveway puck if you beat the undefeated eighth grader. There was a "Name That Tune" booth. It was run by some eighth-grade girls who lowered the lid on a Close N' Play record player.

Patrick and Jimmy stopped by the Presidential Ring toss booth. They bought three rings. They tried to get the rings on President Johnson's nose, but it was too sloped. Then they stopped at the bb gun booth. To win a slingshot, you had to shoot three holes in a target of a Viet Cong soldier from *Life* magazine.

"I wonder where she is," Jimmy said. "She must be over on the other side. I'll meet you later." Jimmy re-adjusted his Cardinals baseball cap to look cool for Cindy and walked off into the crowd. Patrick stood by himself. He paused by the fortune-telling booth. From there he could see the stage where Ebby had danced. He could see the table with the mission money treasure box and the crucifix behind it. He watched a Boy Scout from the ticket table go up on the stage and dump fresh coins into the treasure box. An eighth-grade girl with purple eye shadow and a gypsy scarf was flirting with the crowd.

"Come, get your fortune told, find out which high school you'll be accepted at, Jesuit or public, find out about your love life...."

Patrick gave her a ticket. She looked at him and nodded for him to follow her. They went into a dark room made from a cardboard refrigerator box. She closed the curtain. She turned on a black light. The black light flickered on a Peter Max poster of a guy in star-spangled bell bottoms flying through the sky.

"What do you want to know?"

"Whatever you can tell me."

"I mean what are you interested in ... sports, music, girls?"

"A girl."

"Really, what grade are you in?"

"Second."

"What are those nuns teaching you? I didn't like boys until fifth. What's her name?"

Patrick looked at the Peter Max poster, then back at the fortuneteller. "I thought you were supposed to tell *me* everything."

She flipped her hair around. "I know. I know. I will. I just want to know her name so I can focus."

"Ebby Hamilton."

"I know her. She's the one who kicked the ball over the fence for a dollar."

"Yeah."

The fortuneteller rubbed up the black plastic Eight Ball with her gypsy scarf. Then she pressed her fingers on her temples. "Ebby, Ebby, we want to know about Ebby. Will she be here tonight?" She turned the Eight Ball upside down. The first answer floated into view in the clear plastic window.

"YES."

"She's coming here tonight," the fortuneteller said. "Let's ask it if she likes you."

Patrick swallowed. "OK."

She shook up the Eight Ball and lowered her voice: "Duzzz Ebby love him? Duzzz Ebby like him? Love, like, love, like … tell us Ebby's feelings." She turned the Eight Ball upside down. The answer appeared: "ASK ANOTHER QUESTION."

She leaned back. "You only get one more. What do you want to know?"

Patrick thought about what Dad had said about love and dates not being important. He checked his pocket where the twenty-dollar bill was hidden in the envelope. The envelope was still there. "Ask if I'm doing the right thing."

The gypsy girl lowered her voice. "Is he doing the right thing? Is he doing the right thing?" She shook up the Eight Ball and turned it upside down.

"YOUR HARD WORK WILL SOON PAY OFF."

Patrick started to leave.

"Wait, I can read your palm for another ticket," she said.

"I'm all out of tickets."

"What are you going to spend on Ebby?"

Patrick stepped out of the fortune-telling chamber. He blinked and looked around for Ebby. Some kids yelled "He scores!" by the tabletop hockey booth. Teddy had just scored a goal off the undefeated eighth-grader. Patrick looked around. There were hundreds of kids everywhere, faces moving in and out of view up the long aisles. He didn't see her. He needed to see her. To see her would make him feel more certain. To speak with her would convince him. To "go" with her from booth to booth like on a date would make him understand what Sister Mathilda had said—that *when you love, you do.* He looked at the stage. The mission treasure box was up there. He walked toward the stage steps.

"Your hard work will soon pay off," he mumbled to himself.

He climbed the steps like John Wilkes Booth entering Ford's Theater. The seriousness and secrecy of his mission isolated him from the crowd. The yelling and laughing of the carnival echoed in the distance. He took the stage. His Keds squeaked on the wood floor. The table with the treasure box was ten feet away. He glanced at the crucifix. He glanced at the crowd. No one seemed to care about what he was doing. He took a few more steps. He could see the lid that he would need to open. Then he would put in the envelope. He slipped his hand in his pocket and gripped the envelope. Inside the envelope was the twenty-dollar bill from the bank and the note he had written:

Dear Monseenyor,

I'm sorry for what happened. I'm the girl who stole the Mission Carnival money. I hurd I need to put it back to be forgiven. So when I confess it, that's me, and I'm OK to forgive.

Love,

A Girl

P.S. When I confess it pleese don't ask me anymore questions about it or ask me about this note cause I just want to recover lost ground and move on.

He pulled the envelope out of his pocket. He looked down at the crowd. There she was. Ebby and her parents and baby sister were near the Guess How Many M 'n' M's are in the Jar booth. She looked at Patrick. Her brown eyes looked sad. She seemed to already know what he was doing for her. She seemed to feel the new thing for him. He swallowed. He lifted the lid on the box and flicked in the envelope. He shut the lid. He turned around to hurry off the stage and go meet her. Two Boy Scouts in full uniform were mounting the stage walking toward him.

"Are you Patrick Cantwell?"

"Yes."

"You'll have to come with us. You're under arrest."

"Under arrest? What for?"

"Nothing. It's the jail booth. Somebody paid two tickets to have you arrested. And it'll cost you two tickets to get out."

"But I'm all out of tickets."

The Boy Scouts smirked at each other. "Then it'll be fifteen minutes in the slammer." Patrick walked between them down the stage steps. One Boy Scout blew a whistle to clear the crowd. "Out of the way, prisoner coming through!" They led him past the M 'n' M booth. Ebby looked at him. Patrick shrugged his shoulders to her. Kids threw snow cone slush and stale popcorn at him and chanted, *"Jailbird, jailbird, jailbird...."*

The Boy Scouts locked him in the cell. It was a giant parakeet cage with a wood bench.

"Just tell me one thing," Patrick said.

"What?"

"Who had me locked up?"

"Some kid in a Cardinals cap."

Patrick sat on the bench. He looked around. There was a picture on the wall of Lincoln. The cage bars were pretty clean, except for a few bird dribbles. Patrick wanted to bust out. He needed to tell Ebby everything was OK now. But a Boy Scout guard holding a wooden Pevely Dairy ruler was right outside the cage. Patrick looked at him. It was Raven Hamilton.

"Hey, aren't you Ebby's brother?" he said, "Can you let me out? I need to go talk to her."

Raven looked at Patrick with cold eyes, like he had hated him all his life, even though they had never met.

"You're in jail. Shut up."

Patrick stepped back and looked through the cage bars to see if Ebby was still around. She was out of sight. Next to the jail was the White Elephant booth. Kids with too much faith bought mystery gifts that turned out to be defective toys. On the other side was the cakewalk table. Cakes with swirled icing were on display just out of reach—chocolate, strawberry, coconut sprinkle. The cakes were being tended by the lady Patrick had plowed into outside the bank, the cafeteria lady, Mrs. Heimlich. She put her lips to a bullhorn and pointed it at the ceiling.

"Attention! Everyone, attention. We are ready to begin another round of the cakewalk. Win a lovely cake. We will take the first twelve players to sign up. It costs three quarter tickets. Come to the cake walk!"

Patrick heard a whistle blowing, then the chant, *"Jailbird, jailbird, jailbird...."* Two roving Boy Scouts came through the crowd with another prisoner. They put him in the cage. He was a blond boy from the other second grade class. Patrick had seen him on the playground by the spit pit before, but had never been formally introduced.

"This is a crock of shit," the blond boy said.

They locked him in. He looked at Patrick sitting on the bench, then he grabbed the bars with his fingers.

"Get your fingers off the bars," Raven said, showing he had a wooden ruler.

"This is a crock of shit," the blond boy said spitting on the floor.

Patrick spit on the floor. "This is a crock of shit," Patrick added.

The two prisoners watched the free kids line up for the cakewalk. The cafeteria lady, Mrs. Heimlich, told them the rules. "Soon as we have twelve, you'll go around in circles over there by those numbers on the floor. Some of you will be eliminated, and the last one gets a cake."

"Jailbird, jailbird, jailbird...." The roving Boy Scouts blew their whistle. The crowd cleared a path again. They had apprehended another criminal. It was Jimmy Purvis. They opened the door and pushed him in. He was laughing. Patrick stood up to him.

"Hey, why'd you have me arrested?"

The blond boy looked at Jimmy. "You had him arrested? How does it feel now?" The blond boy punched Jimmy in the stomach. It knocked the wind out of him. Jimmy slumped on the bench wheezing and his Cardinals cap fell off. His face got red. Raven turned around.

"Hey, no fighting or we'll double your time."

The blond boy stood his distance. He leered out at the cakes. Patrick sat on the bench with Jimmy. "You OK?"

Jimmy nodded and held his gut.

"Well, how come you don't buy your way out? You've got all those tickets?" Patrick said.

Jimmy shook his head. His voice was coming in short gulps. "I spent it all."

"On Cindy?"

Jimmy shook his head. "Hell, she's not here. I heard she's home sick. She's got some kind of pro-textile vomiting." He gulped in some more air. "I was so pissed, I blew all my money at the bb gun booth."

The cafeteria lady, Mrs. Heimlich, got back on the bullhorn. "Attention, the cake walk is about to begin. We need two more players to make a dozen, two more players, please come forward."

Ebby ran up to the cakewalk booth. Patrick stood up. Jimmy Purvis stood up. They watched her buy a ticket. Jimmy called out to her, "Hey, Ebby, get me out of prison. Ebby...."

Ebby looked over at the jail. Her eyes met Patrick's. He felt the new thing come over him. She walked closer. Her brother, his Boy Scout vest sparkling with service pins, blocked the way.

"If you want to talk to any of them, you have to wait fifteen minutes," he said.

Her smart eyes looked to the side and read the official rules off the Boy Scout Jail poster.

"Doesn't it say there that I can buy him out?" she said.

"For three tickets, but it's a waste of money. These kids deserve to be locked up."

Ebby looked in the jail. She felt the new thing.

Mrs. Heimlich got on the bullhorn. "C'mon, now, we just need one more player for the cake walk."

Ebby gave Raven three tickets. He put them in a steel combat box. "Which prisoner do you want?"

She pointed toward the cage. "That one."

- chapter thirty-five -

THE CAGE DOOR SWUNG OPEN. The blond boy walked out. He ran to Ebby and hugged her. She laughed and they skipped over to the cakewalk booth. She bought him a ticket. The cakewalk music began. It was a waltz. Ebby held hands with the blond boy and all the other players, as they danced in circles around the numbers painted on the floor.

Patrick and Jimmy pressed their faces against the bars to get a better look. *"Who the hell does he think he is, dancing with her?"* Patrick said.

"I hear they dance all the time," Jimmy said, "They go to that Monday Club."

"The Monday Club?"

As the music warbled, the cake walkers landed on the numbers. Some were in. Some were out. Jimmy sat on the mourner's bench and emptied his pockets of all the prizes he had won at the bb gun booth. Patrick pulled on the bars, looking for a rear exit, but it was no use. There was only a small sliding window on the side for feeding the birds. He watched the cakewalk without blinking. Ebby and the blond boy and a fat girl remained. The fat girl landed on the wrong number. Ebby and the blond boy looked at each other. Patrick watched their hands touch. He started to rattle the cage.

"Hey, Raven, let me out of here. My time should be up."

Raven nodded and pretended to be looking at his jamboree watch, while he wound up his Pevely Dairy ruler and whacked Patrick's fingers. "Now, get back and wait," he shouted. Patrick held his fingers and hopped around the cage, wincing in pain. *"Shit, shit, shit, shit, shit."* Jimmy clapped in rhythm to

Patrick's hopping.

"Shut up," Patrick said.

"Poor Cindy, God, I wish I had a smoke," Jimmy said.

"I wish I had a gun," Patrick said.

"I won this sling shot."

Patrick turned around. "Give it to me."

"No, you can't shoot it indoors."

"You got any ammo?"

"No, just my Super Ball, but—"

Patrick took Jimmy's slingshot and Super Ball and hurried to the feeding window on the side of the cage. Ebby and the blond boy skirted the rules and danced in wide circles around the numbers. The mission carnival crowd watched and clapped. Patrick held the loaded sling shot out the small opening. He pulled back hard on the rubber bands and aimed, trying to get a clean shot at the blond boy. Ebby and the blond boy looked into each other's eyes. To them there was nobody else in the gym. They both felt the new thing. Patrick let the Super Ball fly. It narrowly missed the blond boy's temple and zipped toward the math booth, where it knocked a first-prize replica of the solar system from the winning hands of a Roofus twin.

"We've been forgotten. We've been in here way too long!" Patrick yelled, pacing.

Jimmy shrugged.

"Five more minutes," Raven said.

The waltz music ended. The blond boy bowed to Ebby. She won the cake. Everybody clapped for her. No one had ever won a cake walk so beautifully before. Then the situation went nuclear. The blond boy kissed Ebby—*on the lips*. Patrick turned the bench upside down and Jimmy fell on the floor.

"Damnation to hell!" Patrick yelled.

Out of the crowd came Monsignor O'Day. He was wearing his long black cassock—the same one he'd be wearing in the morning for first confessions. He walked up to Ebby with her parents. Monsignor put his hand on Ebby's shoulder. He said something to her in Latin. She looked at her parents and the blond boy like it was Judgment Day. Monsignor O'Day picked up the bullhorn and addressed the crowd.

"Attention everyone! Attention … I have an announcement to make." Everyone in the gym got quiet. The gypsy fortuneteller leaned out of her box. The tabletop hockey players let go of their control rods. The Rubber Ducky guessers stopped guessing. Everyone turned and looked. Monsignor looked over at Ebby.

"Children, I have some news which I don't like to share, but I have to. It concerns a good Catholic family and their daughter. Their daughter is a lovely girl, an excellent student, a terrific dancer and the only girl to ever kick a ball over the fence for a dollar."

Wild applause broke out for Ebby. The gym shook. But Monsignor motioned for them to stop. "No, please, that doesn't' make this any easier. The thing is … she has to leave our celebration tonight, because of something that happened, and she's taking it very hard, so I want her to know we will always love her. Mr. Hamilton has been transferred to Florida, so tonight is Ebby and Raven's last night with us. They are leaving in the morning. So, let's all join in a song. I think you know the tune." He cleared his throat and sang through the bullhorn to the melody of "Good Night Ladies."

"Good night, Ebby,
"Good night, Ebby,
"Good night, Ebby,
"We hate to see you go…."

The gym full of six hundred students sang and clapped and swayed. The crowd parted as Ebby walked toward the exit carrying her cake. Her brother Raven handed over his Pevely Dairy ruler and his guard post to another scout and left with them. Everyone sang and waved and tried to touch her. Patrick yelled out for her, "Ebby!" But she didn't hear him. Her parents waved thanks. Her mom was carrying the baby girl she got by Ebby jumping in front of the freight train with Patrick. Ebby's eyes got teary. She turned near the door and blew a kiss to the blond boy. Then she started to cry and hurried out. The blond boy started to cry. He ran into the men's room and went in a stall and closed the door to weep hard.

In the birdcage, Patrick and Jimmy watched, as Monsignor signaled the crowd. "OK, just one more announcement. I want to thank you all for participating in the carnival. I guess you know the fun you're having has helped raise money for Catholic charities in forty-seven countries worldwide. The ticket sale booth is now closed, so I want the Boy Scouts to carry the treasure chest over to the priest's house for the final count."

Five Boy Scouts mounted the stage. Four lifted the treasure box to carry it off the stage. The fifth took the crucifix and followed the treasure box. Patrick clutched the bars and watched the treasure box containing his note to save

Ebby leave the gym. Monsignor continued. "And one more thing … We had a little trouble counting the money today, because there were so many pennies. I kept thinking, *where's all the paper money?* Well, we found the culprit. Is Mrs. Heimlich here?"

Mrs. Heimlich waved from behind the cakewalk booth.

"It seems Mrs. Heimlich, our cafeteria director, is so tired of carrying milk pennies to the bank, she asked a student to take out all of the paper money, so Mrs. Heimlich could exchange it for her pennies. Then she had the girl go back upstairs and dump nineteen dollars worth of pennies in there. What a dirty trick! What do you say we have Mrs. Heimlich arrested and put in the jail booth for all the trouble she's caused us?"

Everyone laughed. Then the chant, *"Jailbird, jailbird, jailbird…."* Mrs. Heimlich laughed. The Boy Scouts accosted her and escorted her to the jail. They put her in with Patrick and Jimmy and shut the door. She was laughing. She was gripping the bars. Tears of laughter rolled down her Eskimo Pie face. She looked at Patrick and Jimmy.

"Are you my fellow prisoners?" she laughed. "What are you in for?"

In the men's room, the blond boy wiped the angry tears from his face. He twisted together the fuses of six cherry bomb firecrackers, lit them and flushed them down the toilet.

- chapter thirty-six -

AS SOON AS PATRICK GOT OUT OF JAIL, he ran outside to see if Ebby was still there. But her family Cadillac was pulling away. He stood by the bike rack and watched her taillights turn onto Main Street and melt away. Anything could happen at school at night. He felt like crying and looked around to see if anybody was around. The playground was empty. The gold statue of Mary Queen of Our Hearts was quiet. He would never see Ebby again. He selected a bike from the rack at random, and sent it sailing down the sloping playground, crashing into the fence. He walked over to the gym steps and sat down to cry.

The gym doors flew open. The first wave of six hundred screaming kids ran out. Patrick jumped up and ran onto the playground. He could hear some kind of announcement being made inside.

"OK, KIDS SINGLE FILE, SINGLE FILE, THIS IS NOT A DRILL...."

Monsignor O'Day directed the evacuation from the red, blinking darkness. He shouted through the bullhorn.

"NO RUNNING, SINGLE FILE, WALK SLOWLY TO YOUR FENCE POSITIONS."

Jimmy Purvis ran out.

"What happened?" Patrick said.

"Some kind of explosion in the cafeteria and a big water leak. All the lights are out! Ain't it great?"

Hundreds of yelling kids ran in every direction. Nobody could recall their fire drill fence position. Patrick spotted his brothers. He ran up to them. Teddy was crying. "I dropped the hockey puck I won," he whimpered. John comforted him.

A Webster Groves fire engine pulled onto the lot.

Kids flitted through the strobe lights. Firemen ran down to the cafeteria. The chief announced over the truck speaker: "EVERYONE STAY BACK. GET BACK. GET AWAY FROM THE BUILDING. IF YOU CAN WALK HOME, GO NOW...."

"I'm going with Jimmy," Patrick told John.

"Dad told us to stick together," John said. Teddy was holding John's hand.

"Yeah, I know, but not tonight. I can't walk straight home tonight."

"Remember probation," John said.

Patrick ran off with Jimmy. They ran down the path back by the kindergarten. They made a left and cut through some yards. Lots of kids were cutting through yards. It was a massive escape. They pushed over a birdbath. Patrick and Jimmy stopped to pee on a woodpile. They could see the fire truck lights flashing off by the playground. Nearby they heard boys laughing and cussing. Some boys were up on a garage roof throwing off roof tiles like Frisbees. It looked like a lot of fun. Patrick and Jimmy ran around the side of the garage where a low overhang made it easy to climb up. They got on the roof and recognized somebody. It was Kurt Logan. He saw Patrick and Jimmy.

"Hey, turds." They got busy pulling away the asphalt roof tiles and whipping them skyward. They could see each other's smiles in the flashing fire truck lights. As they flung each tile, they never knew where it would land. Some tiles landed in the yard. Some cleared the fence and landed in the schoolyard by the priest's house. A light came on in the priest's house. It was Father Maligan with his barking German shepherd. He stepped out. "Hey, you birds...." They slid off the roof and ran.

They hopped over fences and ran through yards. They kicked over a trashcan. They threw a tricycle in a bush. They knocked down a concrete garden statue of St. Francis of Assisi. "Take that, you sissy," someone yelled. They kept running. The flashing lights and the commotion of the school were behind them now. They ran across the deck of a built-in pool. Someone threw a wrought iron lawn chair into the deep end. It bubbled to the bottom. A house light popped on. They cut through a break in the fence by an old ash pit and came to a yard with a barking St. Bernard. It slobbered and barked on a trolley chain as they ran past it—just out of reach. They crossed another street and ran down a driveway and behind a garage. Stopping to catch their breath, they beheld the

Missouri Pacific train tracks.

Patrick was beginning to feel better.

They jogged down the backyards along the tracks, knocking over a lawn deer, letting pet rabbits out of a cage. When they reached the train bridge, they all panted like escaped prisoners of war. Kurt Logan passed out cigarettes. They lit up. There were about a dozen parish boys, most of them older. Somebody peed off the bridge on traffic below. Kurt got an idea. He told everybody to hold whatever they had in them. He ran down the embankment and the boys smoked. "I'm gonna die of cancer before I'm eighteen," Jimmy said, laughing. They could hear a trashcan being knocked over, then a dog barking. Kurt ran back up the embankment with a plastic trash bag. He unzipped his pants and went in the bag. Everyone unzipped their pants and went in the bag. One guy had to go number two. He took the bag over to a private area. Then two other guys said maybe they could go number two if they really tried. So they tried. The bag got heavy. Kurt tied a knot in the neck of the bag. He held it up high. The sludgy contents rocked against the plastic seams. He stood on the concrete ledge over the street.

"Guys, there's a little bit of all of us in here," Kurt said.

They waited. And waited. Eventually it came. A glowing Bi-State bus with orange running lights rounded the corner up by the school. It lumbered toward the bridge. Its diesel engine complained as it accelerated over a hump.

"This is it," somebody said.

The bus slipped under the bridge. Kurt threw the bag. Juvenile excrement exploded over the bus windshield. The driver, a big woman who had once braked for a Wolfboy in the same vicinity, flipped on the windshield wipers and kept going.

++++

After a while they ran out of cigarettes. Some kids went home. But Kurt tried to keep the party going with a can of white spray paint he had found in the trash bag. He shook it up and tossed it underhand to Patrick.

"Let's see what you can write on the bridge, turd."

Patrick shook up the can and walked onto the bridge. The gang followed him to the inside of the bridge where the black walls waited like an empty canvas. He put his index finger on the spray button. He wrote the word he first saw on the bridge. He wrote it out in cursive that Sister Mathilda would have been proud of.

Shit.

Somebody else grabbed the can to spray something better. But it was empty. The can was thrown off the bridge. It bounced on the street. Everyone said goodbye. They walked separate ways to go home. The mission carnival was over. Then they heard it.

A train was coming.

The boys looked up the tracks. They could hear it before they could see it. It was a big, groaning freight. The first glint of headlights winked around the curve, flashing up the rail tops like quicksilver. Tree branches and bushes along the line lit up with wild shadows reaching long fingers to grab a boy, any boy. Stumbling and laughing, they ran back across the bridge, dove to the side and waited. The ground shook. The engines roared by. Then the freight cars came, violent and windy. Dust blew in their faces. Nobody even thought about hopping it. It was the kind of train they could only look at and admire, not hop. Kurt stood up and walked into the wind pocket about four feet from the wheels. He flicked his cigarette. It hit a coal car and supernovaed. Kurt picked up some rocks and threw them at the train. It made a ricochet sound. Patrick and Jimmy grabbed some rocks. They let the train have it. They pelted the boxcars. They boinged the oil tank cars. Then a convoy of automobile transport cars appeared. They opened fire. Car doors dented. Paint chipped. Glass shattered. Brand new vehicles would be arriving at dealerships with broken glass hanging from their price stickers. The caboose flew by. Patrick hid like he had the day with Ebby. He remembered how pretty she had been with the wind in her face. But he tried not to think about her. Ebby was gone, and the new thing was dead.

- chapter thirty-seven -

CHRISTMAS EVE DAY

A DEEP SNOW COVERED THE TRACKS and the bridge and the golf course. The fairways and hills were full of kids out of school sledding into the afternoon. It was getting dark. Patrick ran from the house toward the tracks trying to beat a passenger train. It was a fast one, busting down the straightaway, churning up snow dust like a sad daydream. He ran faster and thought about how it would look if he didn't make it in time. What if the train killed him? People would say it was an accident. After all, his Mom had told him to hurry and get his brothers from sledding because of the party. *He must've misjudged its speed,* the police would say. *I had no time to stop,* the engineer would say.

Relatives from way back, and Cousin Jack, and classmates—and maybe even Ebby—would show up at the funeral home. They'd cry and confess that they all should've been nicer to him in life. Jimmy Purvis would confront Ebby next to the casket and tell her she should have bailed Patrick out of jail and not the blond boy at the mission carnival. She would sob on a sofa and never dance with anybody ever again and keep his class picture on her desk until she got old and died. Everything that had happened since he jumped in front of the freight train with Ebby had been like a sour stomach getting worse all year long. It was like sitting in a hot classroom building up to projectile vomiting that only he knew was coming, and he didn't dare raise his hand or tell anyone. His parents didn't know. His brother John didn't know. He never told Jimmy Purvis the truth about everything on his heart. He didn't even tell when he'd made his first confession. He kept secret the twenty dollars he stole from the bank and the vandalism spree after the mission carnival. He felt like a liar taking his first holy communion with all the sins on his conscience, but it was too much to tell anyone. Now, Ebby was gone to Florida, and he was forgotten. He ran up hill through a back yard by the tracks. The train was hurtling forward, throwing snow to the sides. There was just a short sprint between him and death. Maybe he could make it. Maybe he'd get killed. This was it.

He stopped.

He stood still and let the train go by. The windows were yellow with lamplights and he could see revelers drinking and laughing on their way home for Christmas. He thought about Ebby and how stupid he was to jump in front of a train with her. He could've gotten killed. She was somewhere in Florida probably swimming in a pool missing the blond boy. He didn't care about her anymore. He was only pretending about killing himself, just to feel better.

The train passed and just then he heard somebody yelling at him. He thought it was some neighbor saying, *don't cut through my yard*. But he turned and saw it was Sister Jenny.

What was she doing here? He waved to her and waited. Sister Jenny was no longer a nun. She had quit. He was supposed to call her *Aunt* Jenny now. She had on a blue coat and snow boots and a red scarf. She was smiling like she had never been a nun. How she quit the nun business was a family secret. Only Mom and Dad knew the whole truth. But John and Patrick had poked their bath-wet heads down into the clothes chute one night to hear Mom and Dad talking about it in the kitchen. It had something to do with Sister Jenny vanishing from a grocery store field trip. The older nuns thought she'd been kidnapped, because she was younger and beautiful. They called the police. The cops found her a block away in the back row of a movie theater watching *The Sound of Music*. Patrick had never seen the movie, but he heard it was about a nun who falls in love and drops out of the nun business to get married. Apparently, Aunt Jenny was copying the movie the same way Patrick had copied the movie about the Wolfman, and the same way Kurt Logan had copied the movie about the Nazis chasing him on the tracks. Everybody was copying movies to figure out what to do in life.

"Patrick," she said running up to him, "We saw you crossing the street on our way to the party." She acted like she wanted to give him a hug.

Patrick stuck out his arm to shake hands. She shook his hand with a smile. It was still his general policy to never hug a nun, even a former nun. He studied her. She looked different. Not only was she no longer a nun, she seemed awash in the new thing. It was embarrassing. She put her hands on her knees to catch her breath in the cold. "I want you to meet someone." She looked back and waved to her boyfriend. He was a handsome and fit-looking guy in a gold ski jacket. This was the college boyfriend she had left behind to be a nun for a while. Mom had whispered to Dad that he was a non-Catholic like he was a dangerous bank robber. He ran up and said hi and shook hands. He had straight, white teeth and a strong chin.

"What are you doing?" Aunt Jenny said.

"Mom told me to get John and Teddy for the party."

"Are they out there, sledding?"

"Yeah, probably suicide hill."

"*Suicide hill?* Great! Let's go," she said.

She took her boyfriend's hand and they ran across the tracks with her red scarf flapping behind her. Patrick walked after them and thought about how Aunt Jenny didn't belong around the tracks where he had hopped trains and smashed windows and smoked stolen Winstons and done so many bad things. The tracks knew all his sins. But with the snow on the ground, it looked like a different place, as if everything bad that ever happened there was hidden.

Aunt Jenny and her boyfriend waited for him to catch up, and they walked across the fairway toward suicide hill. Dozens of kids were sledding downhill or walking sleds up the slope ahead of them.

"So, I guess you heard, Patrick, I'm no longer studying to be a nun," Aunt Jenny said.

"Yeah."

She looked at her boyfriend and then looked at Patrick. "Chris, here, is a life guard. He rescued me," she said.

Aunt Jenny and her boyfriend laughed, but Patrick didn't get the joke.

"Actually, Chris is a medical student. We met before and used to go swimming. I just wanted to explain to you why I left." She got all serious like she was explaining it to herself, as much to him. "I left because I was trying to do something I could never do. Do you understand?"

"There they are," Patrick said pointing.

John and Teddy were on a sled getting ready to go down suicide hill.

"Is that them?" Aunt Jenny said.

"Yeah."

"Is it safe?" she said.

"It's suicide hill."

"C'mon, I want to try," she said.

Aunt Jenny and her boyfriend jogged up toward suicide hill. Patrick walked behind them. He noticed that Jenny's boyfriend was chasing after her and doing whatever she wanted. *Let's go here. OK. Let's do this. OK. Let's commit suicide. OK, whatever you want.* The new thing can really take you for a ride, he thought. Ebby was probably making Christmas cookies and looking out the window at the ocean as some surfer boys walked by. But that was OK. Patrick was putting her out of his mind. He figured he could find some other girl who reminded him of her. As he walked along, he noticed that all the sledders walking up the hill had stopped and turned around to look back at something out of view. They jumped on their sleds and started going back downhill in a hurry. Then the kids at the top of suicide hill did the same thing. There was nobody left, except for Aunt Jenny and her boyfriend, and when they reached the top, she grabbed her boyfriend's hand and they ran down the other side out of view.

Patrick started running. Something was wrong. He wondered if maybe Teddy and John hit a tree. He made it to the peak of the hill and could see kids below standing around the lake watching the water. Hurrying down the hill, he slipped and fell and got back up and held onto trees along the sidelines for balance. At the bottom of the hill the first thing he saw was Aunt Jenny's boyfriend kicking of his shoes and throwing off his ski jacket and shirt. He dove into an unfrozen corner of the lake. Patrick ran closer. He could see there was some boy out in the deep. There was an empty sled on the ice nearby. It looked like Teddy out there.

"Oh, God, *it's my fault*," he thought. He ran up to the water's edge. Twenty kids were standing around. He looked fast at every face, looking, looking, looking for Teddy. Then he saw Teddy and John standing together. They were OK. They were watching the lake with everybody else. It was some other kid in the water.

"I'm a good swimmer," the boy was yelling.

Aunt Jenny's boyfriend swam out near him, but stopped short and treaded water. Everyone on the shore was yelling "grab him" and "hurry up." But Aunt Jenny's boyfriend kept his distance. "I can swim, but help me," the kid yelled. After a little while, the kid looked exhausted, trying to stay afloat with his wet winter coat and boots on. Finally, he just yelled out "help" one last time and started to go under. Then Jenny's boyfriend moved in and got him.

Everybody on the shore ran to pull them out. The kid was fine, but shivering wet. He never even breathed in any water. He was just beat. He was a first-grader from Mary Queen of Our Hearts. He was on the parish swim team

and supposed to be a pretty good swimmer. The whole crowd went over to the
bonfire and warmed up. Aunt Jenny's boyfriend told the boy to take off his wet
coat and shirt, and then he gave him his own white shirt to wear, which was dry
and hung down to the boy's knees. Aunt Jenny's boyfriend was standing by the
fire bare-chested with his muscles rippling. Patrick looked at Aunt Jenny and
saw she was looking at her boyfriend like he was Superman. The boys were all
excited too, and asking who he was. But he told everyone it was nothing and he
was just another guy. He put on his gold ski jacket and zipped it up. Then he
changed the subject and talked about Santa Claus and what everybody wanted
for Christmas. The boy who almost drowned revived enough to say he wanted
a Rock'm Sock'm Robots and that he knew he would be getting one because he
tore the wrapping paper a little and peeked. Everyone laughed. Patrick looked
at the kid breathing steam and thought about how if he had died, the unopened
gift would have sat there under the tree. It was getting darker and some of the
kids started to go home for dinner. It took about a half hour to get the two
swimmer's clothes dry enough to leave. Aunt Jenny's boyfriend shook hands
with the boy and told him not to go back on the ice to try to get his sled, to just
leave it behind, and go home.

++++

At Christmas Eve dinner, Mom and Dad were astounded as Aunt Jenny
retold the story. Her boyfriend played it down and kept saying, pass the gravy,
or pass the butter to change the subject. Dad wanted to know all about the near
tragedy, and he vowed that it was too dangerous to ever go sledding on suicide
hill again. And he made all the boys promise not to go near that hill, and told
Patrick it would be against the commandment Honor Thy Father and Mother
if he did. Patrick agreed. Mom told Dad to be thankful and make a toast. Dad
only made toasts at the dining room table on big occasions. He got quiet and
thoughtful and he talked about how it had been a year of ups and downs.
Patrick nodded. Dad welcomed Aunt Jenny and her boyfriend, and said he was
thankful for Mom's new baby girl, Elizabeth, who was sleeping, but sad for the
passing of Nana. Then he complimented the boys for being so good after the
Ben Franklin incident and not breaking any laws during their probation. He
raised his glass.

"But I guess what's on my heart tonight is my Pop," Dad said, "He's been
through a sad year with the death of Nana, and though we invited him several

times, he told us he wanted to spend a quiet night at home. Here's to Granddad Cantwell."

Everybody toasted, but it was a depressing toast. Nobody had anything clever to say afterwards. John kept buttering a roll with a sad look, remembering the Beatles concert with Grandad. Teddy rearranged his string beans meekly. Patrick drank his milk from the toast and looked around the table. The candles were flickering and everybody was trying to eat again when the doorbell rang. It was two longs, and two shorts—Granddad's ring.

The table erupted in cheers. Patrick and John and Teddy got up and bolted for the door. Mom and Dad followed with Aunt Jenny and her boyfriend. Patrick opened the door.

"Ho, ho, ho...." Granddad was grinning and wearing a Santa hat and holding a huge box. There was no wrapping paper on it, because he had just bought it and was too lazy to wrap it. It was a Mel Bay drum set.

John yelled the loudest as the boys all shouted, *Yeah! Cool. All right!* Mom and Dad laughed. "So, that's what you were up to," Dad said.

"Are you hungry?" Mom said.

"No, thanks, I already ate at White Castle. Let's set up the drums."

++++

The whole party migrated to the basement, because that's where the old hi-fi set was, and Dad said he didn't want a drum set in the living room, where he likes to think in peace and quiet after work. With some wrenches and pliers, John supervised the project and got the drum set ready. Then he told Mom to put on a good record for the first song. She reached for a Monkees' album, but the record that was in there was Frank Sinatra. Sinatra wasn't any good for drumming. The boys were disappointed. But Mom liked it. It was one of those songs that old people who listened to Big Band Radio knew. John played the drums softly. Granddad danced with Teddy. Mom and Dad danced with baby Elizabeth in their arms. Aunt Jenny danced with her boyfriend. Patrick stood there without a date. He wished things had worked out differently with Ebby. But this was the way it was. He was done with her now. He closed his eyes and pretended she was there dancing with him. He held out his hands a little and moved his feet slightly.

"May I cut in?"

His eyes blinked open. It was Aunt Jenny. She had seen him standing alone and felt sorry for him. Patrick didn't like the idea, but he let her dance with him. She was a fast stepper, and in high spirits. She had drunk some wine, and was really going to town. Here he was dancing with an ex-nun to Sinatra. It was very embarrassing. But, thankfully, the song ended.

"Merry Christmas, Patrick," she said.

"Merry Christmas," he said.

She hugged him close and everyone clapped. Reluctantly, he put his arms around her, and closed his eyes and hugged her for a long, sad time.

++++

Acknowledgments

My mother, who still, though in her eighties, prowls garage sales every Saturday, once bought me a typewriter, and she taught all her kids to wish for that dream that's just out of reach. Here it is, Mom. My late father, a briefcase man who went downtown every day, taught us it's OK to watch cartoons before heading to the office and to keep your sense of humor. I'm sorry he never got to read this book.

A parade of English teachers who wove stories and dispensed writing tips must be mentioned: Sister Gertrude Marie, Father "Killer" Kane, Jeanne Smith, Carl Evola, Tom Auffenberg, Susan Tierney, and, most of all, David Carkeet.

A comic novelist, Carkeet taught fiction writing at the University of Missouri-St. Louis. That's where I met him as a student. Like a nuclear scientist handling dangerous compounds, Carkeet showed his students how to write comic fiction, or at least blow up the lab trying. It was for his 1993 novel writing class that I wrote a rough draft of *Never Hug a Nun*. The novel ended up entombed in a basement box as I got busy with life and career. An email from Carkeet eighteen years later urged me to dust it off, rework it, and submit it to Blank Slate Press, resulting in this book, suitable as a drink coaster or fly swatter.

Blank Slate Press was probably skeptical at first of the project, but after seeing the first fifty pages, asked for the rest of it. Then due to an error in judgment, they agreed to publish it. This good news came at just the right time, as my self-esteem was so low I had bought a batch of used horse trophies at a garage sale for twenty-five cents each (with my mother along) just to cheer me up.

Editor and Publisher Kristy Blank Makansi made many helpful suggestions, hacking out gangrene sentences, and encouraging me to round out the narrative here and there so that the novel in my head would end up on the page. It's been a pleasure to work with this independent publishing house that has won national awards and appears to be going places.

Thanks also to Kristy's husband Jason Makansi, Marketing Director Jamey Stegmaier, and Zoe the intern. They all read the book and suffered no permanent effects.

Oh yes, I can't leave out Kristy's brother who supplied the endearing cover photo of himself. What a snappy dresser. I never met him, but he looks like a mischievous kid deep down, who could be in the gang—once he loses that tie.

About the Author

A reporter with KMOX radio since 1995, Kevin Killeen has confused listeners for the past ten years with his regular morning feature, *A Whole 'nother Story*. Killeen has also authored the annual KMOX Holiday Radio Show, an original comic play with a holiday theme, for the past fifteen years or so. In *Never Hug a Nun*, Killeen's first novel, he attempts to escape his declining faculties by casting his mind back to the days of his youth when he spent long summer hours on the train tracks or hanging out at the Velvet Freeze and wishing he were a teenager.

A 1982 graduate of University of Missouri-St. Louis, Killeen studied fiction writing under comic novelist David Carkeet who corrupted him with thoughts of getting published some day. Married with four children, Killeen enjoys asking his kids—again—to please, pick up their shoes. He also keeps busy by moving the sprinkler around a dying lawn and going to garage sales on Saturdays with his mother.